CULM ROCK,

The Story of a Year:

WHAT IT BROUGHT AND WHAT IT TAUGHT.

BY
GLANCE GAYLORD.

BOSTON:

Innes and Niles,
Stereotypers and Printers,
37 Cornhill, Boston.

CONTENTS.

CULM ROCK.

CHAPTER I.

THE OLD STONE HOUSE.

CULM ROCK was a wild place. You might search the coast for miles and not find another bit of nature so bare and rent and ragged as this. So fiercely had the storms driven over it, so wildly had the wind and waves beat, that the few cedars which once flourished as its only bit of greenness were long ago dead, and now held up only bleached and ragged hands. Jutting out into the sea, the surf rolled and thundered along its jagged shore of rock and sand, and was never silent. It would have been an island but for the narrow strips of sand, heaped high and ridgelike, which bound it to the main land; and this slender bridge, it often seemed, would be torn away by the ravenous sea which gnawed and engulfed great tracts at once, and yet heaped it higher and broader in the next storm. Beyond, on the firm and unyielding land, the pine woods stood up, vast, dim, and silent, stretching away into the interior. So, with the great dark barrier of forest behind and the waste of shining sea in front, Culm Rock seemed shut out from all the rest of the world. True, sails flitted along the horizon, and the smoke of foreign-bound steamers trailed against the sky, giving token of the great world's life and stir; and there were Skipper Ben and the "White Gull" who touched at the little wharf at Culm every week; but for these, the people — for there were people who dwelt here — might have lived in another sphere for aught they knew or were conscious of what was transpiring in the wonderful land which lay beyond the stretch of sea, and between which and themselves the "White Gull" was the only means of communication.

Do you wonder that people could spend their lives here, die, and never have seen the world without? There were only a dozen houses, — poor, racked, weather-beaten things, nestled on a bit of sand on a far corner of Culm, — inhabited by fishermen and their families. They were rough, hardy folk, but ignorant, and with only ambition enough to get their living out of the great sea, and a poor and scanty enough living at that. Skipper Ben brought them molasses and calicoes down in the "White Gull," and took their fish in exchange; and if he told them a bit of news from the great city and the greater world, it was all very well. If he failed to do this, it was all very well too.

Back of the fisher huts, the rocks rose high and dark, and quite hid the pine woods and the isthmus of yellow sand, and everything that could make Culm at all cheery or pleasant. This eminence was Wind Cliff, and served as a land-mark for all the sailors whose path lay along the coast. Around this the gulls were alway flitting and screaming, and their nests were everywhere in the crev-ices of the rocks. Bald and gray it rose, scarred and rent with storms and age, and so steep as to be almost inaccessible. It fronted the north-west, and from its sharp tip the rock sloped south to the sea, and held in one of its great hollows down by the shore a house — such a house as you would not have looked for at Culm — with walls of stone and tall, ancient chimneys and deep-set windows, like eyes looking forever at the sea.

It was so dark and weather-beaten that at first sight you might almost fancy it to be but some quaint, odd shape which the rocks had taken, by dint of the stress of winds and waves beating upon them for long ages. But a house it was, and made by human hands, and human beings dwelt in it. At night the red light from its windows streamed out upon the water, and in many a dark and tempestuous watch had Skipper Ben guided the "White Gull" into port through the friendly gleaming of this beacon. For a long period of years the old house had stood empty and tenantless, the windows and doors broken and gone, the wind sweeping through and the rain beating in, and everything but the stout walls and chimneys a ruin. The superstitious fishermen would not inhabit it, and told tales of smugglers and pirates who made it their haunt, with other fanciful stories which always seem to linger about the sea, and in which there was not the faintest shadow of truth. Desolate and neglected, it stood there year after year, till, one day, Skipper Ben brought down carpenters and masons on the "White Gull," and straightway they went at work upon the old house. Doors went up, windows went in, a piazza pushed itself out towards the sea-front, and there was great bustle and activity about it for weeks. Then the laborers went away, and when the skipper came again, he brought, instead of grocer-ies and store-cloth, a great quantity of fur-niture, the like of which the poor people at Culm Rock had never seen, and with the furniture came the master of the new house — a sorrowful, bowed man — and his housekeeper, a thin, wrinkled negro woman.

Then the smoke curled out of the great stone chimneys once more, the light streamed from the windows at night, and the fishermen and sailors rejoiced that at last the old house had found a tenant and no longer yawned bare and empty. The "White Gull" came more than once with a cargo for the master of the stone house, who, the skipper told the Culm folk, "was a mighty rich man, but the down-heartedest chap he'd ever cast eyes on. Why, man, he just sot lookin' over the rail the best part o' the way down, with his eyes in the water, and said no more nor a stone. What ye think? Now lookee here, men, let me give ye a bit o' advice. Don't ye go to pesterin' him with yer talk and yer questions; fur he's diff'rent make 'an I be, an' 'twon't do. Let him alone, an' keep yer own side o' the Rock."

The skipper's word was looked upon with respect by all the fish-folk, and they heeded his advice. So, in consequence, the owner of the stone mansion was undisturbed, and lived in the greatest seclusion. He never came within the limits of the little village, and whenever he was seen, it was only as pacing slowly along the shore. He passed the fishermen as they were hanging up their seines in the sun without heeding them, or acknowledging their respectful bows. The old black housekeeper came down to the village sometimes after fish or gulls' eggs, but went her way without satisfying the eager questions with which the women plied her. So one year passed away, then a second, and the master of the stone house was still as much a mystery to the poor fishers as ever. He rarely walked upon the sand, gave them not a look if ever they chanced to meet, and living, apparently, for no one but himself, took not the slightest interest in their welfare, cared naught for wreck or disaster on the shore, and seemed always stern and sorrowful.

No company ever came down on the "White Gull" to visit this strange and silent man, and he had no friends, apparently. Skipper Ben brought stores for him occasionally, and sometimes a letter; but this last event was a rare one, and the man seemed to have little more communication with the great world out of which he had come than did the humble Culm fishermen. With winds and storms, the third year rolled around, and the master of the old house was still as much of a recluse as ever; but the Culm people had ceased to regard him with any interest, and the man led a most solitary life, hardly seeing a human being, other than his housekeeper, from month to month. Do you wonder what could make him so stern and sad? Here is his story:—

One sweet and golden summer day, a man stood by the bedside of his wife,—he, crushed and heart-broken; she, faint and dying, but calm and loving and comforting. She held his hand, and whispered brokenly such words as she could only hope to comfort him with; and the last faint whisper which trembled on her lips was, "Oh, Richard, don't fail — don't fail to — to find Him and cling to Him, and come — come up — too." And with that she was dead. And the man left the bedside, and went out into the summer fields, where the birds were flitting and the bees droning and the wide earth seemed brimming with life and joy, and prayed that he might die too, since she was gone. But the birds sang on as joyously as ever, and the sun shone no less brightly because of the sorrow in the earth, and after his first tears were shed, his heart began to grow hard and bitter, and he put away the dying whisper, and went back to the dear dead face, cold and stern. His friends came to console him, but he would not listen, and after it was all over, and the gentle face hidden forever under the brown earth, he began to think of fleeing to some spot where he might find rest and quietness, and hide himself from all thoughts of the dear one who had left him, smothering his sorrow, and living as if she had not been. "I have been robbed," he said, bitterly; "all my happiness has been stolen from me. I can't seek Him; I will not. Oh, if there is a kind and merciful God, why has he stricken me? why has he taken all the joy out of my life? why has he left me without a comforter in the world?" So, without seeking for a Comforter, without striving to "find Him," as the dear voice had whispered, he turned away and strove to crush out the love and the tender memories which haunted his heart, and most of all that dying whisper which said, "Don't fail — don't fail to find *Him.*"

Grown suddenly stern and morose, Richard Trafford looked about him for a refuge where he might flee from all society, and most of all from the spot where *her* presence seemed yet to linger. He discovered wild and solitary Culm Rock, and purchased the old stone house. Here, he thought, with the everlasting sound of the sea in his ears, with all tne wildness and barrenness about him, and apart from the rest of mankind, he would bury himself, and forget all the bright and happy days which had passed. He left his friends without giving them any clew to his whereabouts, and with faithful old Hagar, who persisted in following him, took up his abode by the sea. But do you think his sorrow lessened? Do you think he found peace and happiness again? He carried his hard and bitter heart with him, and there was no happiness to be found by the sea. One year after another rolled away until the three were gone, and still he was wandering along his own thorny path, bowed with his sorrow, sighing and lamenting for the bright form which had left him, and still deaf to its whisper, "Find *Him*, and come up too." He walked on the sands, lonely and desolate; he paced about the great rooms of the stone house, oppressed and heavy-hearted; he shut himself up in his library and pored over books in vain. His sorrow clung to him, followed him everywhere; his heart was stubborn and bitter and rebellious. Perhaps he despaired of ever losing the burden, for one day he brought out a portrait, wrapped and swathed with great care, and, tearing all the veilings off, gazed once more on the sainted face which he had not looked upon for three long and heavy years. He did not hide it again, but hung it upon his library wall, where the tender face and calm and loving eyes looked down and almost melted him to tears.

He wondered how he could have kept it veiled and hidden so long. He wondered if those three years had not been spent in vain, unless it were to learn that he could not crush out his sweet memories if he tried.

He sank down into his chair as he thought of this, and going back over the three past dreary years, remembered what a weary blank they were, thought, with a heavy sigh, what a shipwreck his life had been, and how he was now floating about without rudder or compass or anchor, merely a drifting wreck. And as he sits there in the sunshine which streams through the wide, high old window, we will see him for the first time.

CHAPTER II.

LETTERS.

RICHARD TRAFFORD was a man of forty; but his hair was tinged with gray, and grief and wretchedness had worn heavy lines in his face. As he sat in the library this September afternoon, looking up at the portrait on the wall, he seemed almost an old man. The room was wide and high, with tall oaken bookcases at either end. Two great windows, before one of which he sat, looked out upon the sea and the white line of foam curling upon the sand. The waves were but mere ripples this calm afternoon, but from the shore there came up a ceaseless, steady murmur that made itself heard in the quiet of the room; and by and by Trafford's eyes turned from the calm face above him and looked out seaward. White and shining lay the vast expanse, with here and there the faint film of a sail upon the horizon. Nothing to be seen but water and the great dome of sky and the little spit of yellow sand where the tide was murmuring. How many sunny afternoons he had thus looked out upon the sea, vast and gleaming! How many lonely afternoons and long, weary nights he had listened to the slow chanting of the tide, watched it creep up the sand with its puffs of thick foam, watched it as it slowly receded and left its burden of weed and shell behind! Flowing and ebbing forever, alway at its work, in and out, in and out, through storm and shine, through night and day, it seemed to mock his own idle, useless life, and reproach him with its never silent voice. Of what use, he wondered as he sat there, was such a life as his? To-morrow the tide would be at its work again, the ships go on, the sun shine warm and bright over all, — and he? For him to-morrow would be but the repetition of to-day; the same dragging hours, the same apathetic poring over books, the same half-hours at the organ with the music-books, playing sad melodies which accorded well with his own sombre feelings. He looked up at the portrait and sighed; remembered the dear one's dying words, and thought, "I might have found Him once; but it's too late now. All that passed away a long time ago, and now, — it's only to plod on and on, year in and year out, till the end." And what then?

There came a soft rap at the door.

"Come in, Hagar," said he, heavily, without taking his eyes off the sea; and then the door was pushed open, and a head, surmounted by a great yellow turban, looked in.

"Somethin' fur you, Mas'r Dick," said the owner of the turban, without coming in, however.

"What is it?" said Trafford, abstractedly.

The door opened wider, and the old housekeeper entered. She was bent and thin, with great wrinkles in her forehead and face, and wherever a tuft of wool peeped out from under the fanciful head-gear, it showed quite gray; but her step was quick and firm as she went across the floor to the figure by the great window.

"A letter, Mas'r Dick," said she, standing by Trafford's chair; "dat yer old skipper brought it. Said he brung it straight from de city."

"Ben Tate?" asked the master.

Hagar nodded assent. "Said ye was to hev it dis yer afternoon, sure," said she; "'twa'n't no letter to be lyin' 'round in dem Culm huts, so he cum up here wid it hisself. Be it frum Hastings, Mas'r Dick?"

Hagar had lived in the Trafford family from childhood, and Richard had grown up to manhood under her eyes, had married, and she went to live with the young people. She had seen the wife fade and die, and the husband grow stern and gloomy, and out of solicitude and affection had clung faithfully to him through all fortunes. It would seem, to hear her talk, that she never had quite realized that Richard Trafford, the man of forty, was any other than "Mas'r Dick," the boy whose smartness at school, and whose popularity among his companions, had always been her boast and pride. Gray and worn he was getting, gloomy, sad, even harsh at times to her, yet he was only "Mas'r Dick," and her own little boy, for whom she must watch and care to the best of her ability. Now, as she queried where the letter might be from, she dropped down in a chair a little way from him, and waited till he should see fit to answer her question; for could there be a paradise on earth, it would have been represented to Hagar by Hastings,—that great city where their old home had been, where her own childhood had been spent, and where all the friends of her kin and color dwelt. It was a hard matter to tear herself away from them all and follow Richard Trafford to dreary Culm Rock; but, with some tears and sighing, she had said to her people, "Yer don't know nuffin about it. Ye habn't got any 'Mas'r Dick;' so how ken ye? 'Tain't in dis yer old heart to let de chile go off sufferin' all by hisself, now! Bress de Lord, I'll stick to de poor boy, an' keep him frum jes' worryin' his life out." So here she was in her old age, away from all her people, yet happy because it was to serve "Mas'r Dick."

Trafford took up the letter,—a large,

thick one, bearing the marks of the skipper's great fingers on its envelope, and smelling of fish, as if it had performed its journey in company with herring and cod, — and said, "Yes, Hagar; it's from Hastings, of course."

The old housekeeper lingered, looked at the master in hopes that he would bid her stay, and then, as he tore open the letter with a moody face, went slowly out, closing the door softly behind her.

The handwriting was unfamiliar, and Trafford wondered where it came from, feeling vexed that it should have arrived at that moment; and so began to read an emphatically business letter: —

"HASTINGS, Sept. 7th.

"*To Mr. Richard Trafford, of Culm Rock:*

"SIR, — I am sorry to be under the painful necessity of informing you of your brother's death. The Rev. Oliver Trafford died the 15th of March last, leaving me as the executor of his estate. He was anxious to see you till the very last; but as we had no clew to your whereabouts, and only discovered your place of residence by accident a short time ago, that pleasure was denied him. He left one child — a boy of fourteen, or thereabouts — for whose welfare he was much distressed. He often expressed it as his desire that, should you ever make your appearance, this boy might be received by you as your own, and, indeed, left written statements to that effect. There is, also, among his private papers, a sealed letter for you, which, I doubt not, contains some such request. The boy, I am happy to say, is not likely to prove a burden or trouble to you, being obedient and all that could be desired. He is smart and sprightly, and quite a favorite in the circle in which his father moved, and from my own acquaintance with him (very intimate during the past six months) can assure you that he will prove anything but a poor acquisition.

"As to the estate, I am sorry to say that Mr. Trafford left but little of value,—enough, perhaps, to educate the boy; but, as I hear you are a gentleman of fortune, this, I presume, is a matter of very little moment. I shall be happy to show you your brother's accounts at any time, and to have the honor of answering any inquiries which you may be disposed to make. I enclose a note from your nephew. Awaiting your decision in the matter, I am, sir, your most obedient servant,

"THOMAS GRAY.

"Room 8, at No. 67 Court St."

With a gloomy face, Trafford laid down the lawyer's letter, and took up his nephew's. He did not remember ever having seen the boy. He was, most likely, a crazy, boisterous lad, that would be forever in mischief, and bring the house about their heads. As for having him at Culm Rock, it was too preposterous a thought to be entertained for a moment. He had decided at once how Mr. Gray's letter should be answered, and felt too indifferent to care about reading his nephew's. What did these things matter to him? Yet, after a time, he thought better of it, and took up the note again, saying to himself, "I'll read it, if only because it's poor Noll's boy;" and opening the missive, found therein the following frank boy's letter: —

"HASTINGS, Sept. 7th.

"DEAR UNCLE RICHARD, — I don't know what to say to you — it all seems so strange and awkward. Mr. Gray said I was to write, however, and send the note with his; so I am trying. It is such a long time since I saw you that I've forgotten your face, and I think you must have forgotten that there was such a person as myself in the world. Papa died almost six months ago, and he said all the time, at the last, 'Go for Uncle Richard!' but I didn't know where you were, and Mr. Gray could not find out till a short time ago; so papa died without seeing you. I don't know what he wanted to say, but he told me that I was to live with you and be your boy; and Mr. Gray says the papers say the same thing." Here the writer had evidently faltered, and been at a loss how to proceed further with intelligence which it, apparently, was very irksome for him to disclose; but he continued with, "There are only you and me left, and I am sure I would like very much to be your boy and live with you, as papa said; but — but I don't know — I mean — Well, I can't say it, Uncle Richard, but I mean that I wish I might know what you thought about it first. I wouldn't like to come, you know, unless you liked, — unless you were *glad* to have me. Mr. Gray has all papa's business to settle, and I suspect he wants to get me settled, too, somewhere, pretty quick; and so, if you please, I hope you won't mind whatever he may say about me, and only do just as you like about giving him permission to send me. I can find a home somewhere, if you would rather.

"My name is Oliver, — Noll, everybody calls me; I'm almost fifteen, and have always been at school in Hastings, and papa used to give me lessons beside. Is there a school at Culm Rock? I do wish you could have seen papa, dear Uncle Richard, he longed so for you when he died; but there is a letter for you among his papers, which will be sent to Culm Rock, if I do not come to bring it. Mr. Gray will tell you all about me, I suppose, and the affairs besides; so I will stop.

"Your nephew,

"NOLL TRAFFORD.

"— And don't mind what Mr. Gray says, please, and only do as you like."

Richard Trafford finished this letter with something like a grim smile on his lips. "The boy has got the true Trafford spirit," he said to himself, "and some of Brother Noll's gentleness, I fancy. Ah, Noll was always a happier man than I!"

He read the boy's letter again, wondering what made it seem so bright and pleasant, and feeling vexed with himself for doing it. Why should he care for this boy or this boy's letter? Had he not fled to Culm Rock to escape all knowledge of what was transpiring in the world without, — to forget friends and kin, if that was possible? He looked up and met the sweet, grave eyes of his wife looking down into his, and read something there which made his eyes fill and his lip quiver.

"Ah," he sighed, "why did I not try to follow after?" And with this thought in his heart, he rose and stood by the window, looking down at the crawling tide. His thoughts came back to the boy, presently, and with another grim smile upon his face, he remembered what a dull and dreary place Culm Rock would be for a lad of fourteen. He would soon tire of it, and be glad enough to go back to Hastings, he fancied. If he was a wild boy, he should go back on the return of the "White Gull;" if he could be tolerated, he might stay till he tired of it. It was poor Brother Noll's boy, after all, he thought, and he could not make his heart quite hard enough to refuse him a home. So, when Skipper Ben returned to Hastings with his next cargo of fish, he carried a letter hidden away under his pea-jacket, and this was what it contained: —

"CULM ROCK, Sept. 12th.

"*To Noll Trafford:*

"Come; you are welcome.

"UNCLE RICHARD."

CHAPTER III.

ON THE "WHITE GULL."

THE breeze was crisp and fresh that morning, and the skipper anxious to set sail. Everything was in readiness on board the "White Gull," but still its master did not give the word to cast off, and stumped up and down the deck, muttering and grumbling to his mate.

"Allus jes' so!" he said, wrathfully; "these town folks never up to time. Think on't, Jack, that 'ere lawyer, Gray, promised to get the youngster here a good half-hour afore sunrise! Here it's sun-up already, and this breeze won't last forever, nuther."

"Why don't ye go 'long 'thout him?" queried Jack Snape from his seat on a bucket.

"Would, ef 'twa'n't fur that pesky lawyer!" growled the skipper; "an' 'tain't every day ye can get a passenger fur the Rock, nuther. Mought as well take what passage-money he can, a fellow mought, Jack."

The mate of the "White Gull" began to whistle, and fumbling in his pea-jacket brought out a pipe and tobacco, with which he proceeded to console himself. Skipper Ben took a few more impatient turns up and down the deck, and sat down at last in grim despair, while the wind came in strong, steady puffs, and the craft rocked and swayed gently on the swell of the tide. The city behind them was hardly awake yet. Its roofs and steeples loomed through a veil of haze or smoke which hovered over and clung about the towers, and only a faint murmur told of the stir and bustle which were presently to reign. On the wharves a few early drays were rumbling down after their loads of merchandise, and one or two vessels had left their moorings, and, taking advantage of the favorable breeze, were standing out to sea, which fact did not at all add to Skipper Ben's good-nature.

"Here they come," drawled the mate, putting up his pipe; and then a carriage came rattling down the wharf, stopping in front of the "White Gull."

"Come at last, hev ye?" shouted the skipper, gruffly. "Call this a half-hour afore sunrise, squire?"

"Well," said the lawyer, looking at his watch, "I thought we were prodigiously early. Driver, put these trunks aboard in a hurry, since the skipper is waiting; and — Noll, are you ready?"

The skipper left his craft and came to bear a hand with the trunks, looking askance, meanwhile, at the boy who had got out of the carriage and stood on the wharf's edge, surveying the "Gull."

"Hope you'll have a good run, skipper," said the lawyer, as the baggage went over into a cavernous aperture in the deck; "fine breeze, I should say. Have a good care of this passenger of yours, man."

"Ay, squire, we'll manage. Can't stop fur words from ye this morning; should ha' been a long piece down the coast afore this time o' day. Bear a hand there, Jack!"

"Good-by, Noll," said the lawyer; "keep up a stout heart, my boy, and don't forget your city friends. You'll have a fine run down to Culm, and you must send me a line back by the skipper. Good-by!" and Mr. Gray got into his carriage and rolled back toward the city.

Noll Trafford stood leaning against a great post and looking after the lawyer's carriage with a slight choking in his throat, till the skipper's gruff "Get aboard here, lad!" warned him that the "Gull" was about to cast off. Slowly the wharf glided away, and the little coasting vessel stood out into the channel. The city spread itself out behind them, a long maze of brick and slate, with spires and domes showing dimly through the blue haze which wrapped them about. On the far, watery horizon lay a belt of vapory clouds which presently began to rend and tear and float off in ragged masses, and then a great red sun gleamed through and made a golden roadway across the sea, and transformed the misty fleeces of vapor to wonderful hangings of amethyst, streaked with great threads of scarlet.

"Jes' sunrise!" muttered the skipper; "make the best o' this 'ere breeze, eh, Jack?"

"Ay," drawled the mate, "we'll catch it afore long, skipper."

The city's old cold front suddenly gleamed out in vivid gold, the spires grew rosy in the first rays of sunlight, and, all its dimness and dulness gone, Hastings lay gleaming and glowing in the fair morning light like some vision of fairy-land.

Noll Trafford, sitting on a great bale of merchandise near the stern of the "Gull," gazed at the city, slowly sinking and fading in the sea, with a feeling somewhat akin to homesickness. It had never looked so bright to him before as at this moment of his departure from it, and he was leaving behind a great many friends — all his school acquaintances, all the scenes and haunts that were dear to him — to go — where? He hardly knew, himself, but his bright fancy had pictured Culm as some pleasant little sea town, where there would, perhaps, be a great beach to ramble upon and hunt for minerals and shells, and where he would soon make plenty of new acquaintances. And Uncle Richard he had pictured to himself as a gentle, kind man, — grave, perhaps, but who would love him and try to fill the place of his own dead father. So, with these bright visions filling his mind, it was little wonder that he turned from the stern, after Hastings had faded into the merest blue dot on the horizon-line, and looked forward to the time when the journey's end should be reached, with happy anticipations. Before them lay the vast and boundless sea, with no trace of shore or island save a low blue belt in the south, like a cloud, and the "Gull" began to pitch and toss somewhat with the great ocean-swell. Skipper Ben, having got well in the way of the breeze which was carrying his vessel steadily before it, began to regain his good-humor. Sitting on the top of a cask, he puffed away at his pipe and soliloquized to himself about his passenger, who sat regarding Jack Snape's movements at the helm with much interest. The skipper had three or four boys at home,—great sturdy, brown-faced, stout-armed fellows,—between whom and this fair-faced, curly-headed boy there was little resemblance, he felt. "Town breedin', town breedin'," muttered he; "it's curi's what it'll make of a lad. This chap'll grow up with his head full o' le'rnin' into a lawyer or parson or somethin' like, and my lads'll be skippers like their dad, with no le'rnin' to speak on. I'll warrant this lad could get off more book-stuff in five minutes 'an mine ever heerd on." His eyes followed the boy as he went out to stand by Jack's elbow and ply this slow-witted gentleman with quick, eager questions. He was slender and rather tall for one of his age, but lithe and agile, as the skipper noted. "One o' mine could jes' trip him with a turn o' his hand," thought he; yet he regarded the lad with a mixture of kindness and respect, after all. There were other things in the world beside bone and muscle, he remembered, and when the boy came slowly along the deck, after a fruitless attempt to coax the mate into conversation, he put out one of his big red hands and stopped him. Noll looked up, inquiringly.

"Goin' down to Culm for a bit o' vacation?—to git scarce o' the books, eh?" queried the skipper.

"Vacation? Oh, no," said the boy, quickly; "I'm going there to live,—to have a home."

The master of the "Gull" came near dropping his pipe with amazement. "*You* live at Culm!" said he, incredulous; "what ye goin' to live in?"

It was Noll's turn to look amazed. He

suddenly faced the skipper, saying, very earnestly, "What kind of a place is Culm Rock, anyhow? Isn't it a town?"

A broad grin stretched across the old sailor's face, then he laughed aloud. "Did ye hear that, Jack?" he cried; "here's a lad what's goin' to Culm to live, an' he wants to know ef it's a town!"

"'Twon't take him long to find out arter he gets there," drawled Mr. Snape.

Noll turned away and walked to the stern, thinking the skipper was a very uncivil fellow to laugh at his ignorance, and sat down again on the bale, secretly ill at ease on account of these sailors' words. What kind of a place could Culm Rock be?

All around the boundless waste of waves flashed and glittered under the sun, and the "Gull" sailed steadily on her course with not a fleck of land in sight,—nothing around but the vast blue of the sea,—above, only the great azure arch of sky. It was a new and strange sight to Noll Trafford. He lay on his back on the bale, and looked up into the wonderful depths of the blue dome, where no clouds sailed, and speculated about his destination. Somehow, the bright vision of a pleasant sea town with a shining beach of sand and pebbles had faded, and in its stead there was doubt and perplexity. Was it only a rock, as the name suggested, and no town? However, Uncle Richard was there, and that was one comfort; and perhaps the skipper was only joking, after all. He wished, though, that he might know what to expect; he wondered why he had not thought to ask Mr. Gray before starting. He lay a long time listening to the rush of water about the vessel, a strange and unusual sound to his ears. By and by a brawny hand touched his shoulder, and a gruff voice said, —

"Lookee here, lad!" Noll turned about and saw the skipper. "'Twa'n't manners in me to laugh at ye, I 'low," said he, good-humoredly; "but 'twas droll, ennyhow. Hain't ye never been to Culm afore?"

"Never," said Noll.

"An' ye don't know nuthin' what it's like?"

"No; how should I?" said his passenger; "I didn't know there was such a place in the world a month ago."

The skipper looked incredulous once more. "An' now ye goin' there to live!" he exclaimed; "why, there ben't but one house there fit fur such as you, an' 'tain't there ye're bound, not by a long shot!"

"But *one* house! Whose is it?" cried Noll, eagerly.

"Why, it be one Trafford's, one o' the strangest—" A sudden expression in the boy's face checked the words on the skipper's tongue, and the truth began to dawn upon his slow brain. "Great fishes!" cried he, falling back a step or two, "ye ben't goin' *there?*"

"Yes," said Noll, as quietly as he could. "Why not?"

The skipper gave him a long, steady survey, and then stumped away across the deck without another word, leaned over the rail, and began to whistle. Noll looked after him, half determined to follow and demand what he meant, yet half dreading to learn that all his visions were a great way from the truth. Perhaps it would be better to wait, he thought; night would bring the journey to an end, and then he should know all. So he did not follow the skipper, but kept his seat, while a great many shadowy forebodings crept into his heart, and he began to look back over the trackless waste which they had come, and wish, almost, that he was back in dear old Hastings — in the old home where papa and he had spent so many happy hours — and that Culm Rock was a myth. The sun rose royally up to noon, and odors of dinner began to ascend from the hatchway. Noll had a dinner of his own somewhere in a basket, which he brought forth and ate on the bale which served him for a seat, enjoying the novelty in spite of the anxious speculations concerning his new home in which he could not help indulging.

After dinner the skipper was in better humor than ever, and took his turn at the helm. Noll, wandering about the deck, stopped to watch him, whereupon the master of the "Gull" good-naturedly answered all his questions, and even allowed him to take the tiller a few minutes, laughing the while at his white hands that could hardly grasp it.

"Wish ye could see my lads' hands!" he said; "could take both 'o' yourn in one uv 'em, an' not know they was holding anything. But you'll have browner paws afore ye leave Culm!"

"Of course!" said Noll, "for I'm going to get Uncle Richard to teach me to row, — I can swim now, — and I'm going to be around the shore half the time."

"Likely enough, likely enough!" said the skipper, meditatively; and when Noll had passed on, he muttered, "It's a pesky shame fur the lad to be sent off and cooped up on the Rock! Don't know what he's comin' to, nuther. I'll be blamed ef I ain't sorry for the boy!"

CHAPTER IV.

DISAPPOINTMENTS.

IT was late afternoon when land loomed up blue on the horizon. Mr. Snape had taken the tiller, and Noll stood leaning over the rail by him, eager and watchful for the first look at Culm. "Mought as well wait a bit," Jack Snape had drawled out; "we sha'n't get there fur a long while yet, lad."

But the boy chose to keep his place,

and kept his eyes unweariedly on the distant point for which the "Gull" was making. Yet it was but tiresome watching, after all, and the brisk breeze seemed to have failed them somewhat, for the vessel's speed had sensibly diminished.

"He'll be glad 'nough to look t'other way arter he gits there," muttered Skipper Ben, between the whiffs at his pipe; "my lads 'ud think they's killed for sartin to be shut up there a week." He got up at last, knocked the ashes out of his pipe, and disappeared down the hatchway, returning presently with a spy-glass, which he carried to his passenger with, "Lookee here, boy, take this an' make out what ye ken. 'Tain't much ye'll see yet, but mebby ye'll get a look arter a time." He sat down again, looking at the boy's face from time to time, and wondering if this sending him to Culm Rock was not some of that Lawyer Gray's work. The skipper had not a very high opinion of lawyers.

Slowly, slowly the blue point began to take shape, and Noll's glass brought it to his eyes all too faithfully. The skipper saw the eager look and the warm color which had been on his face fade slowly out as the "Gull" drew nearer and nearer the journey's end, and the warm-hearted sailor waxed indignant. "Mought ha' told him what ter expect, anyhow!" he muttered, shaking a great bale with his brawny hands as if it had been Lawyer Gray's shoulders.

The "Gull" stood in toward shore. First, the pine woods, vast and sombre, showed themselves; then, a little way on, Culm Rock came slowly into view, bald, ragged, and desolate. Noll's face was very grave, but he kept his place and said nothing. Slowly the curve of the shore unfolded itself, a long line of yellow sand, length after length of scarred and jagged rock. The sound of the surf came faintly out, sounding over the ripple of water about the "Gull's" prow. Not a sign of life, as yet, had showed itself. The vessel kept steadily on till, at last, the whole great breadth of the Rock lay before them, rising huge and massive out of the sea, and, in a sheltered hollow on the shore, a great stone house stood up, gray and weather-beaten as the cliffs about it.

"Is that the house?" Noll asked, turning to the skipper, and laying down his glass.

The old sailor nodded assent, thinking to himself that he had never seen it look darker and gloomier, and wondering what the boy thought.

"Aren't you going to stop?" Noll asked, as the "Gull" kept on, and the stone house dropped astern.

"Goin' round to the landin'," explained Mr. Snape; "'tain't good moorin's till ye git half a mile fu'ther round. Ye'll git ashore pretty quick."

Under the cool and heavy shadow of the Rock they crept, coming out of it at last into the full glory of the sun's setting. All the west was aflame, and the sea glowed and sparkled like molten gold. Even the wretched little Culm fish-huts looked almost fair and comely in this flood of light.

Noll Trafford scanned the little wharf, where a motley collection of men were gathered, with a quick-beating heart.

Which of them could be Uncle Richard? Would he give him a kind welcome? The boy's spirits began to rise somewhat under the influence of the broad, cheerful glow of sunshine and the speedy prospect of meeting this uncle who was to be as a father to him. The remembrance of the gray old house under the shadow of the rocks around the curve of the shore still lay somewhat heavily on his heart; but if Uncle Richard were only glad to see him, all that would not matter, he thought. He stood by the prow as the "Gull" moved slowly up to the wharf, eagerly scanning every face that was watching the craft's motions. A sudden pang of disappointment chilled him from head to foot, for among that idle, shiftless-looking group, there was not one whom he could possibly mistake for his uncle. They were all fishermen, dull-faced, dirty, and out at their elbows. Some frowsy, ill-clad women had come out of their houses, and, with children clinging to their skirts, looked on with idle curiosity.

So this was Culm Rock! Noll's bright fancies had all fled, and his heart was suddenly very heavy. He looked back across the sea toward Hastings, longingly, and thus verified the skipper's prediction. If Uncle Richard had only been there to greet him, he thought, chokingly, it would not have mattered so much, but now, it was all forlorn and dreary enough.

"'Tain't much uv a town arter all; is it?" drawled Mr. Snape, with a broad grin on his thick features.

"Shut up, Jack!" growled the skipper. "Can't ye see the lad's got all he ken weather?" Then he turned to Noll, proffering his rough sympathy. "Sorry fur ye!" he said. "Culm ain't the place for the like o' you, an' what ye cum here fur, I can't see. But keep a stout heart, lad, an' rough it out best way ye can; ain't no other way now."

"I'm going to," said Noll, with an effort; "I won't mind after a little, I guess. Good-by, skipper;" and he stepped out on to the little wharf among the fish-folk, who made way, regarding him curiously.

"Keep 'long up the shore," called the master of the "Gull" after him, "and you'll cum to the house afore long. I'll send yer trunks up by some o' these 'ere good-fur-nothin' Culm folks. Good-by, lad!"

The skipper watched the boyish figure walking away up the sands, and remarked to his mate, "Ef I knew that was some o' Gray's work, I'd jes' like the fun o' bringin' the ole chap down here on the 'Gull,' an' lettin' him loose to browse on the rocks,—jes' to see how *he'd* like it!"

Noll walked briskly, trying to keep up good heart by whistling and humming snatches of tunes, looking back over his shoulder at the wonderful gleaming of the west, and the queer picture which the fish-huts and the group of idlers made, with the "Gull" lying by the little wharf, her cloud of canvas yet unfurled and its shadow gleaming white as ivory in the depth of water on which she floated. At his feet the tide was murmuring. How far and vast stretched the sea! What a minute atom of earth was Culm Rock, compared with the boundless waste of waves which compassed it about! Bending over all, the evening sky lay cool and serene, flushed, where it met the water, with lovely stains of color. Noll was but dimly conscious of these things as he hurried on, because his heart was filled with conjectures about the stone house and the friend he was to find there. The disappointment of not finding his uncle awaiting him with a warm greeting still lay heavily on his heart; and as he passed the curve of the shore, and the stone house came in sight, his quick pace slackened, and he walked but slowly.

There was no one visible on the piazza. All the doors and windows were closed, though the evening was warm and mild.

The boy wondered if his uncle was absent. Perhaps, he thought, with a little thrill of pleasure, that, after all, was the reason why Uncle Richard had failed to meet him.

A thin blue film of smoke crept up from one of the tall chimneys, telling him that some one was within the gloomy old structure, which, it seemed to him, looked much more like a grim fortress than a *peaceful* dwelling. Not a blade of grass or anything green flourished about it; all was rock and sand and stranded kelp.

His heart beat fast as he went up the piazza-steps, and noted how his footsteps echoed in the silence. He rapped on the great oaken front-door. No one answered the summons. He rapped again, wondering if Uncle Richard was really gone, and his heart began to grow heavy again, as it had done upon his first disappointment at the wharf. The lonely voice of the sea stole up to his ears, and he turned about to look. Twilight was fast settling down upon it, and already the far horizon was hidden; but along the shore the waves shone and gleamed white-ly. Noll's first pang of genuine home-sickness came upon him here. It seemed as if he had not a friend this side of the wide, dark sea.

This second summons met with no better success than the first. Noll turned away, went back down the steps, and there stopped to look about him. He discovered some straggling footprints in the sand leading around the corner of the house, and these he followed for lack of a better guide. They led him to a long, low projection from the main body of the house, a kitchen it appeared to be, and here he found a wide-open door, from whence came the strains of a hymn half chanted, half sung. Noll rapped. The singing ceased. A slow step came across the kitchen floor, and a voice said, "Bress us! who's dis?"

Noll looked up at the wrinkled black face framed by a great yellow turban, and said, —

"I'm Noll Trafford. Didn't — didn't Uncle Richard expect me?"

Old Hagar threw up both hands crying, shrilly, "Bress de Lord! is dis Noll Trafford's boy?" and then stared blankly at him.

"Yes, if you mean Uncle Richard's brother," said Noll, still very sad-hearted; "and wasn't he looking for me at all?"

"Bress ye, honey!" said Hagar, recovering her senses, "he didn't say one single word to me 'bout ye! Dun forgot it, I 'spose. But don't ye stan' on dem yer steps another minnit; come right in, honey. I'll see Mas'r Dick dis instant."

Noll followed her into the little kitchen, where on the hearth a fire was crackling and flashing its red flicker over the walls. He sat down on a rough wooden bench by the door, wondering if his uncle could really have forgotten that he was coming, and feeling not all light-hearted, while Hagar clattered away to "see Mas'r Dick." She came back pretty quick, saying,—

"You's to go right in to de lib'ry, chile, right in jes' as soon as I git dis yer candle lit;" and getting down on her knees she puffed away at the coals and burned splinters till she succeeded in coaxing her tallow candle to burn. She got up, came back to where Noll was sitting, and holding the light close to his face, looked down at him long and steadily.

"Bress de Lord!" she said, stroking his curly hair, "you's de bery picter ob yer father. 'Pears like 'twas him I see'd dis minnit 'fore me! Did ye drop down frum de sky, or what, chile?"

"I came down on the 'White Gull,'" Noll answered.

"Well, now!" said Hagar; "an' why didn't yer father come too?"

"Papa? Oh, why—papa is dead," said Noll, with a little quiver in his voice which he could not possibly prevent, he was so lonely and homesick.

Old Hagar gave a shrill wail and set her candle down.

"Now don't tell me dat!" she cried. "Mas'r Oliver dead? Well, well, honey, we dunno nuffin on dis yer Rock? De whole ob creation might cum to an' end, an' we nebber hear on't. An' you's all alone now, chile?"

"Yes," said Noll, feeling at that moment as if there were never truer words spoken.

"An' you's come down to lib wid yer Uncle Dick?"

"Yes."

"Well, bress de Lord fur dat!" said Hagar, joyfully; "couldn't a better ting happened to dat yer man, nohow. Jes' what he wants, — a boy like yerself, wid yer own father's face. An' did Mas'r Dick know ye's comin'?"

"Yes, he knew," said Noll; "he — he told me I'd be welcome. Do you think I am?"

"Why, yes, honey! What made ye ask dat? Yer Uncle Dick is a strange man, an' ye mustn't mind if he don't say much to ye, an' — but come right in de libr'y, chile, fur he's waitin' fur ye. Come right along; I's lit de lamp in dar;" and taking up her candle, she led the way.

"Don't yer mind dis ole hall," said Hagar, by way of apology as they entered a long, bare, chilly corridor; "nobody comes here but me, an' I don't mind. It's only my road frum de libr'y to de kitchen. *He* nebber comes out here."

From this hall they passed into the dining-room, where stood a supper-table very plainly spread.

"Mas'r Dick didn't eat nuffin to-night," said Hagar, glancing around as she clattered on. At one end of the dining-room they came to a door which the old housekeeper softly opened.

"Go right in, honey," she said to Noll, in a whisper; "he's dar," and then turned away.

Richard Trafford sat by one of the great bookcases, reading. The lamplight fell full upon his worn and sorrowful face. He did not hear the door open, did not hear Noll's light step, and was first conscious of the boy's presence when two arms were suddenly clasped about his neck, and a voice, trembling with a mixture of joy and sadness, cried, "Oh, Uncle Richard!"

CHAPTER V.

THE FIRST EVENING.

RICHARD TRAFFORD, a little startled, unclasped the boy's hands without a word, and held him off by one arm. Full in the light he held him, gazing in his face long and keenly. Then he said, "So this is Noll!"

Oh, how coldly the words fell upon the boy's heart! How the stern voice and the keen gray eyes chilled him! Not a word of welcome, after all,—only those four chilling words. The boy's disappointment was so great, his heart so lonely and homesick, that he stood with downcast eyes, before his uncle, to hide the tears that glittered in them, and could not answer a word. Trafford released his nephew's arm with a sigh. The boy was the very counterpart of his father, of Brother Noll, he thought,—the same fair, high forehead and curling locks, the same deep blue eyes, the same eager, impetuous manner. This resemblance touched him somewhat; he noted, also, that the boy's lips quivered a little, and so said, in a kindlier tone,—

"You're very welcome to Culm, Noll. Are you tired with the journey?"

"No—yes—some, I mean," stammered

poor Noll, winking hard to keep the tears back.

"And you'd like some supper, I dare say," continued his uncle.

"Yes, by and by," the nephew managed to answer.

A silence fell upon them here, — long and deep, — in which the eternal murmur of the sea stole in. Trafford's eyes did not move from the boy's face; and at last he said, taking his hand, —

"You're wonderfully like your father, Noll, — in more ways than one, I hope. Can a lad like you ever be contented in this old house?"

"I — I hope so, Uncle Richard," Noll replied, mocking these words, however, by a very despairing tone.

Trafford smiled grimly. "He's weary of it already," he thought; "and who can wonder? Noll and I couldn't have endured it at his age, I suppose." Then he added aloud, "If you tire of it, Noll, you shall have liberty to return to Hastings whenever you choose. You're not to stay against your will, remember. You may find it lonely and dull, perhaps; if so, I leave you to go or stay, as you choose."

The tone in which this was spoken was so sad that Noll ventured to look up into his uncle's face. The gray eyes had lost their stern light, and looked very sorrowful.

"I—I will never want to go back, Uncle Richard, if you would like me to stay," he said, quickly.

"Ah, you don't know what you say, Noll," Trafford answered, stroking the boy's hair; "it's a lonely place. For a boy it is horrible. Even I sometimes find it but a weary resting-place. Ah! wait and see, wait and see. I've little hope you'll stay longer than a month."

At this Noll's heart gave a leap of joy. "Do you really *hope* I'll stay, Uncle Richard?" he cried.

Trafford looked at the boy's eager, searching face for a second, then answered, "Yes, if you can be contented." This was hardly such an answer as Noll craved, yet it made his heart lighter. Perhaps it was only Uncle Richard's way, he thought, which made it seem as though he was not welcome. The old black housekeeper, he remembered, had warned him not to mind it. With this thought, his heart grew somewhat more cheerful, and he began to take a brighter view of things. He noted the tall cases of books and the open organ, and unconsciously these evidences of taste and refinement made the thought of dwelling in the stone house more acceptable. If Uncle Richard would only care for him, he thought, all the rest would not matter.

Trafford let go his hand, saying, "Go and get your supper, Noll; Hagar will show you. Then, if you like, you can come back."

The boy took two or three steps toward obeying, then, as if remembering some duty unperformed, turned and came back.

"I had forgotten the letter, — papa's letter, — Uncle Richard," he said, drawing the missive from his pocket. "Would you like it now?"

Trafford extended his hand without a word. Noll placed the precious letter therein, and walked away, looking back at the door to see that his uncle had broken the seal. Not till the boy's footsteps had died away did the uncle look upon the hurriedly-traced lines which the note contained. The letters were feebly made, hinting of the weakness of the hand which traced them. This was what he found:—

"My dear Dick,—I write this to you from my dying-bed, not knowing that it will ever reach you, or that you are even upon the face of the earth. If ever you *do* return,—if ever you receive this, be kind to my poor Noll for my sake. Make him your own,—he'll love you,—and make him such a man, before God, as you know I would have him.

"If he has disappeared, look him up,

search for him, and cherish the boy as my precious legacy. And, dear Dick, look well to yourself. A man needs much when he lies where I am lying. We ought to have been more to each other these past years, not living with a great gulf, as it were, atween us. This and the thought of my boy is all that weighs upon me now.

"And, dear Dick, till we meet again, farewell, farewell. O. TRAFFORD."

A sudden mist came across the reader's eyes, a sudden throb to his heart. Brother Noll! the blithe, warm-hearted, once precious brother! he who had astonished all his friends by studying for a minister, and who, with all the fervor of youth, had devoted every talent and energy to the sacred cause. How he had loved him once! How proud and happy he had been at his success! And here were words, his last thoughts on earth, breathed from the very depths of his heart, and thrilling with love for himself and this boy. They stirred the man's heart as it had not been stirred before since that dreary afternoon when all the joy and sunshine fled out of his heart and left it so cold and bitter. He had not realized before that Brother Noll had really ended his pilgrimage, and passed out of the earth, which, to himself, was such a weary abiding-place. Now, with the last whispers of that dear heart before him, the whole bitter sense of his loss came upon him, and he covered his face, sighing heavily. Back came the remembrance of the long and happy days of boyhood, with visions of the shining meadows where they strayed together; with visions of careless, joyful hours, when they sailed and fished and hunted the woods for purple grapes and glossy nuts; with visions of those calmer days when they grew up to manhood together, — Noll always bright and brave and loving, and a check upon his own wilder spirits. Now he was gone; and all the years to come could never again bring joy so deep and love so everlasting. Yet, true and dear to the last, he had breathed his life out in one sweet message to himself, confiding his love and this boy to him as a precious legacy. Trafford almost groaned when he thought of his loss. Oh, what a cruel thing was Death! A fierce, pitiless robber, seeking for the loveliest and brightest, it had lain in wait, all his life long, despoiling him of whatever he set his heart upon, he thought, and leaving him wrecked and desolate. He had thought that no death or sorrow could ever move him again; yet here was his heart aching as wretchedly as ever. Was there no place in the wide, wide earth where such wretchedness could not pursue? He had hoped to find it in this wild and barren Rock; yet here sorrow had crept in, bitter and poignant as in the busy city.

Trafford rose from his chair, put away the message from out of his sight, and sat down at his organ to still the pain in his heart with the charm of its music.

Noll had had his supper, and was sitting, sad and solitary, by Hagar's fire in the kitchen. He would wait a little, he thought, before going back to the library, that Uncle Richard might have time to read his letter. He wondered what its contents could be, and wished and hoped that papa had written some message there for himself. Would Uncle Richard tell him if there were? he wondered. Then his thoughts went back over the sea to Hastings, and there came up such pictures of the dear old home there, and the faces of his school friends flocked before him so vividly, — Ned Thorn's in particular, — that he could look about him only through tears that he strove in vain to banish.

Hagar had gone out with the candle, so the kitchen was quite dusk, save where the fire flared scarlet light on the wall and ceiling. Suddenly, in this silence, there stole in a heavy throbbing, like the beating of a great, muffled heart, and with a slow and solemn movement, rolled and swept in long chains of sound through the house, till, at last, a clear, sweet, flutelike warble broke in and ran up and down, seeming to wind in and out with the heavy undertone. Hagar came in just then with her flaming candle, and began to rattle about among her pots and kettles.

"What is that?" Noll asked, quickly, as the strains kept stealing in above the clatter which the old negress made. It had startled him at first, coming so suddenly, and corresponding so well with the gloom and mystery which seemed to fill the house.

"Bress ye, honey!" said the black old figure, stooping over the cooking utensils on the stone hearth, "don't ye know? Dat's Mas'r Dick at his organ. He sits dar mos' times at ebenin', an' 'pears like I ken jes' tell his feelin's by de music he makes. Sometimes I ken hear it jes' as sad as nuffin ye ken think ob, an' sometimes it's singin' as ef 'twas 'live and 'joicin.' It dun make ye homesick?" queried Hagar, dropping her dishcloth and looking up into the boy's face.

"No," Noll answered, with a sigh, "'tisn't the music. It will all be gone in the morning, I guess," and tried to look his cheeriest.

"You's tired out, chile," said Hagar, with ready sympathy; "better go to bed. I's been makin' ye one in de room jes' side o' Mas'r Dick's. Bes' room in de whole house!"

The music had ceased, and Noll left his seat and went groping his way along the dark, echoing hall, through the dimly-lighted dining-room to the library-door. Entering, he found his uncle still seated before the organ, but with his head bent forward upon the music-rack, and apparently lost in deep thought, for he did not look up till Noll stood beside him. Trafford made a faint attempt to smile, and asked,—

"Could Hagar find you anything fit to eat? We can't live here as at Hastings. The sea brings us our food."

Noll said something about not being hungry, and presently Trafford asked, with the stern and gloomy look upon his face,—

"Did you know that Brother Noll, your father, did a very unwise thing when he put you into my hands?"

Noll started at the strangeness of the question, and the bright color came into his face.

"Do you mean that papa did wrong?" he asked, quickly.

"Yes, so far as your good is concerned. I can be no companion for you. You would have got more good anywhere else than here."

"Don't say that, Uncle Richard!" Noll pleaded.

"Why not?" Trafford queried, not unkindly; "it is the truth."

"Papa said that you — you —" There was such a choking in Noll's throat that he could get no further, and stopped, looking very much distressed. Trafford took the boy's hand in his own.

"My boy," he said, huskily, calling him by that title for the first time, "I'm but a poor wreck at best. I can teach you no good, and God knows I wouldn't be the means of putting a shadow of evil in your heart. Your father says, 'Make him such a man, before God, as you know I would have him.' He asked too much, Noll. Why, boy, I can't rule myself." Noll said not a word. Uncle Richard was getting to be more of a mystery to him than Culm Rock had been. "And," continued Trafford, "we will leave the matter thus: you shall be at liberty, after the first month, to go or stay, as you like. If you go, it shall be to stay away forever; if you stay, it shall be at your own risk. Do you understand?"

"Yes, Uncle Richard."

Trafford saw the boy's lips quiver again, and turned quickly away; the face was so much like his dead brother's. Noll came to him pretty soon, said "Good-night," and went away. Hagar guided the boy up to his room, bidding him good-night with many assurances that "'tw'u'd be pleasanter to-morrow, 'nough sight!" and left him to himself. The stars shone brightly over the sea. Noll could not read his Bible verses that night, for the familiar, precious gift of mamma was locked in the trunk away round the shore at Culm; but he prayed with all the stronger longing for the Saviour's pity and help; and then from his bed by one of the great windows, lay listening to the moaning of the tide below, which seemed the saddest, lonesomest sound he had ever heard. And his heart ached too.

CHAPTER VI.

CULM SIGHTS.

WHEN Noll awoke the next morning, the sun was shining brightly in. It was not until after some long minutes of yawning and rubbing his eyes, that he comprehended where he was; then, with some chills of disappointment, he remembered, and bounded up to look out the window. The sea lay rippling, cool and fresh below. Here and there faint trails of mist floated and hovered over the waves, but the breeze was fast tearing and blowing them away. With a feeling of delight, he saw on the far horizon-line the white film of shadowy sails. It showed that there was life and stir somewhere, he thought, and it was pleasant to think of them as bound for far-off Hastings. Then he remembered Skipper Ben and the "White Gull," and wondered when he would return; and then Mr. Gray's note had not been written, he recollected.

"Well," thought Noll, "I'll find time for it to-day, I guess. I wonder if my trunks will come this morning? and— When am I to begin my studies, and who am I to recite to?" This last thought had not entered his head before. There was evidently not a school of any kind upon Culm

Rock, and of course Uncle Richard was the only person capable of teaching him anything. "I wonder if he will offer to teach me?" Noll thought in perplexity, "or shall I have to ask him? I can't do that! he's so cold and stern; and besides, I don't believe he would like the trouble. I wonder if I am to grow up like those dull Culm people?" He dressed himself, thinking busily enough of a dozen troublesome matters which had already sprung up to puzzle him, and with these in his head, went down-stairs. He found the dining-room at last, after getting into three or four empty, unoccupied rooms, and there found Hagar putting the last dishes upon the breakfast-table.

"You's lookin' brighter, honey," said she, gleefully. "Didn't dis yer ole woman tell ye so? Ki! I knowed how 'tw'u'd be las' night."

"It *does* seem pleasanter," Noll admitted; "and where's Uncle Richard?"

"Mas'r Dick? He's in de libr'y; goin' to call him dis minnit. Breakfas' dun waitin' for ye both, honey; an', bress de Lord! how much ye looks like yer father dis mornin'!" and Hagar caressed the boy's hair with her skinny old hands, muttering, as she gazed affectionately in his face, "You's de bery picter ob him,—de bery picter!"

So Richard Trafford thought as he answered the old housekeeper's call and entered the dining-room where his nephew was waiting with a cheery "Good-morning, Uncle Richard." The boy's sunshiny face, somehow, made the great room brighter, Trafford thought, and Hagar bustled about and poured the coffee with a lighter heart than she had had since leaving her people at Hastings.

"Good morning, Uncle Richard," Page 92.

"Jes' what's been lackin' de whole time!" she thought to herself; "Mas'r Dick wants somethin' he ken love and talk to. 'Pears like dar'll be a change in dis yer ole house afore long, de Lord willin'." It was such a long time since the old negress had seen a young face, or heard the pleasant accents of a young voice, that she made various pretexts for lingering in the room while the two sat at the table, and though it was for the most part a silent meal, yet it was a wonderful pleasure to see Noll eat, Hagar thought. And when the two had left the table and gone to the library, she soliloquized, "Nebber thought I'd see a day like dis yer, agen! Wonder what Mas'r Dick t'inks o' de boy? Bress de chile! if mas'r don't take to him, 'pears like he'll nebber take to nuffin. Be like habbin' poor Mas'r Noll's face afore him de whole time, an' ef he ken stan' *dat*, athought lubbin' him, I's 'feard he's dun got colder'n a stone, de whole ob him. You jes' wait an' see, Hagar!"

Noll followed his uncle from the breakfast-table into the library, hoping that he would at once say something about his books or studies, or at least hint what plans he had made concerning himself. It would be a great deal pleasanter, Noll thought, to have Uncle Richard dispose of him, even in a stern, cold way, than to do nothing at all with him and remain indifferent as to whether he studied or grew up in ignorance.

But Trafford had relapsed into one of his gloomy, absent moods, and took up a book as soon as he reached the library, without a look or word for Noll. The boy stood by one of the great windows and looked out on the sea, striving to drown his disappointment by thinking of other matters. When he had tired of this, and found that disappointment was long-lived, and would not be drowned, he loitered by the bookcases, reading the titles, now and then peering into a volume and looking over its top at his uncle, and thinking him a very cold or else a very forgetful man. When he had made the tour of the room several times, and was about to go out in despair, Trafford looked up.

"Noll, did you wish to speak to me?" he asked, abruptly.

The question came upon Noll unawares.

"Yes, if—if you were not too—too busy," he stammered. "I thought—I hoped you would say something about my books—my studies, I mean, Uncle Richard."

"What about them?"

"Why, whether I were to study with you, or by myself, or how; and whether I am to begin now, or wait a while," said Noll, wishing that his uncle would look less keenly at him.

Trafford leaned his head upon his hand and reflected a little. At last he said,—

"You will wait, Noll, till your month is up. There would be no use in beginning studies which, perchance, may end in so short a time. If, at the end of four weeks, you conclude to stay, then we will talk about study. Till then, you will wait."

Noll's blue eyes said, as plainly as eyes could, "Don't mention that month again, Uncle Richard!" but his tongue was silent, and he acquiesced in this decision by a nod of his head.

"You can fill up the time," continued his uncle, "as you like. You had best make yourself acquainted with the Rock before you decide to stay here. You will hardly explore it all in one day, I think;" and with this Trafford turned again to his book.

Noll found his hat and went out, determined to keep a brave heart if Uncle Richard *was* cold and gloomy. If there was no other way, he would *make* him love him, he thought, though how that was to be done he had, as yet, but a very slight idea. He went through the dining-room, and from thence found his way to the broad front piazza which faced the sea, and where, the previous evening, he had stood so lonely and homesick. Everything looked much cheerier to him now, and he ran down the sand, in front of the house, to the water's edge, resolved to see the bright side of everything which pertained to gray, barren Culm. There were stranded shells and bright-hued weeds on the wet, glittering sand, which made Noll's eyes sparkle with delight.

"Wouldn't Ned's eyes open to see these!" he thought, "and wouldn't the dear old fellow like some for his museum! I'll gather a whole box full and send them up by the skipper some day."

Thinking of the skipper made Noll remember his trunks, and he wondered if the "White Gull" had continued her voyage farther down the shore.

"There's a whole month to explore and pick up shells in," he said to himself, "and I'll take this forenoon to go around to the landing and see the skipper, if he's there."

With this thought, he started off, hoping to find the "Gull" still lying off the little wharf. The skipper seemed almost like an old friend, already; and, however rough he might be, he came from Hastings, and this fact alone made the boy long for a sight of his face. So he hastened along the sand, toward Culm, with an eye and ear for everything which he passed. Great boulders, all green and fringed with sea-weed, were strewn everywhere, — in the yellow sand of the beach, in the line of the tide and waves which whitened themselves to foam, and murmured hoarsely against them. In some places the great mass of the rock came down so near the water's edge that only a slender path of pebbles was left between it and the waves. In high tide, Noll thought, this narrow way must be quite covered, and he wondered why the sea did not carry it quite away. But in other places the beach was broad and smooth, quite wide enough for many horsemen to ride abreast. This morning the sea was peaceful and calm. Neither did it look so vast and illimitable as on the previous night. The tide was going out, stranding great quantities of glittering weeds and all sorts of curious objects, the sight of which made Noll's heart glad; but, without stopping to examine or preserve them, he hastened on, hoping to soon catch sight of the "Gull." But in this he was disappointed. No sooner had he passed the curve of the shore than he saw that the skipper and his craft were gone. There were his trunks to see to, however; so he kept on, though at a slower pace, wondering if those dull-looking fishermen could tell him when the "Gull" would return.

Not half so fair or comely did the dozen houses look as in the gold of sunset. Such racked, weather-beaten dwellings Noll had never seen before. It was a mystery how they could ever stand in a high gale. Not a solitary vestige of anything green was there to enliven the barrenness. Long lines of seine were stretched upon stakes, and dangled from the sides of boulders upon the shore. In the sand some dirty-faced children were playing, who got up and ran away at his approach. A little farther on he came upon two fishermen dividing a basket of fish. They looked up, stared, and nodded respectfully.

"When did the skipper go?" Noll asked, pausing.

"Ben, ye mean?" asked one of the men, suspending his labor to take a more leisurely survey of the questioner.

"Yes, Ben Tate," said Noll.

"Afore sunrise," said the other. "Did ye want the skipper, lad?"

"No, not particularly. When is he going to stop here again?"

"Ben? Why, he comes Mondays and Thursdays, he does," said the fisherman; "ye'll find him here day after to-morrow, lad, — early, too, mos' like."

"Can you tell me where he left my trunks?" queried Noll.

At this question, the men looked perplexed. "Do ye mean boxes like?" they asked, after a time.

Noll was astonished at this lack of knowledge, but managed to explain to the two what he meant.

"Ye'd best go up to Dirk Sharp's," said one; "the skipper leaves much with Dirk, he does, an' ye'll be like to find 'em there."

"Back o' the wharf, lad,—back o' the wharf Dirk lives," the other called to Noll, as he walked away.

Dirk Sharp's house was rather smarter than the others,—at least, it was in better repair; but the look which Noll caught of its interior, as he stood rapping by the open door, sufficed to destroy any anticipations of industry or thriftiness which he might have formed from the dwelling's exterior. Dirk was a great broad-shouldered, slouching fellow, with a general air of shiftlessness about him. At Noll's summons, he came lounging out of an inner room, and, catching sight of the boy, said,—

"Lookin' for yer trunks, lad? The skipper said ye was to hev 'em las' night, shore; but ye see," pulling up his sleeve, "as how I got a cut what's hindered," displaying a long, bloody wound upon his arm. "Ye sh'u'd ha' had 'em, lad, but for that, as the skipper said. But ef ye ken wait till the men get back from their seinin' — Ho! there be Bob an' Darby now," he exclaimed, as he spied the two whom Noll had just passed.

"Ahoy there, lads! here be a job fur ye!" he cried to the fishermen.

The two left their work and came up to Dirk.

"Here be two trunks to go 'roun' to the stone house fur this lad," said he. "Ef ye'll shoulder 'em roun' the shore, yer welcome to what the skipper left fur't. What ye say, lads?"

"We'll do't fur ye, Dirk, seein' yer cut," said the one who was called Darby. "Where be the boxes, man?"

Dirk led them into the inner room,

from whence they presently emerged, each with a trunk on his shoulder, and, bending with their burdens, started up the shore.

Noll followed slowly after, wondering why they did not use their boat, instead of enduring such back-breaking toil. It struck him that he had never seen such dull, apathetic faces as these Culm people had. Such utter shiftlessness as everything about the cluster of tumble-downs betokened he had never imagined. Perhaps all this dreariness and desolation made itself more keenly felt because the boy was just from the city, which teemed with life and bustle and energy. In its poorest quarter he had never seen such a lack of tidiness as the interior of Dirk Sharp's house presented. He followed the slowly-plodding trunk-bearers up the yellow sand, wondering if there was such another wretched, desolate, and forlorn place as Culm Rock in the whole wide earth.

CHAPTER VII.

HOW THE MONTH WAS SPENT.

THEY were a long time in getting to the stone house. Before they passed the curve of the shore, the sun was well up in the sky and beat down with fervid rays upon the sweating, toiling fishermen. Noll rejoiced when the trunks were safely landed in his room at the top of the stairs, and the men had taken their departure, each with a piece of silver in addition to the skipper's fee. It seemed to him that there was no bright side to the life over in those wretched Culm huts. If there was, he could not see it. It puzzled and perplexed him to imagine how human beings could live in such ignorance and apathy of all that was transpiring about them; and the sights which he had seen in the miserable, tumble-down village left a very disagreeable feeling in his heart. Somehow, his hitherto blithe spirits were dampened by this morning's walk, and he thought the great bare Rock would be a great deal more endurable if the fish-huts and their inmates were only off it. True, it would be much lonelier, but that was far more endurable than the sight of such shiftlessness and ignorance. He wondered if Uncle Richard ever went among them, and whether he really knew what a degraded people they had got to be. If he did know, Noll thought, it was very strange that he did not try to lift them up, teach them something, or, at least, have a school opened for the children. Papa, he thought, would have done something for them long ago. There would have been a little schoolhouse and a teacher. A new wharf, he was sure, would have taken the place of the rickety old thing; and by degrees the women would have learned thrift and neatness, and the men energy and industry. To be sure, it seemed a great deal to do for such dull, apathetic people, who seemed not to have a particle of energy and ambition about them; but papa, he thought, could have done it, and *would* have done it, had he lived here as long as Uncle Richard. He remembered a little sea-town, where they had lived before dwelling in Hastings, how wretched and dirty and ignorant the fishermen were, and what a great change for the better came over the place through his father's efforts.

But now papa was gone, and Uncle Richard? The man was so much of a mystery to Noll, as yet, that he did not know whether there were any hopes of his setting himself to the task of lifting the Culm people out of their slough of wretchedness; but he hoped that his uncle would see and realize what needed to be done before another year had worn away. And if he did not? Why, then they would have to go on in their old way, he thought. He wished that he might do something toward the work; but, then, how could he? He had no money, and no means of getting any, and he was not fifteen.

Noll put away, or tried to do so, all thoughts of the Culm people and their life, and went to writing the note which Skipper Ben was to carry to Mr. Gray on his return to Hastings. When it was finished, he unlocked his trunk, took a look at the thumbed, worn little Bible which had been mamma's; at the familiar covers of his school-books, which brought up a hundred visions of pleasant, happy hours in the great, buzzing schoolroom, — wondered if he should ever know such joyful moments again, — it seemed quite an impossibility, now, — and took up, one by one, the keepsakes and knick-knacks which his boy friends had given him on his departure. There was the new ball which Sam Scott had given him, — how Sam *did* love ball-playing! — and which was now not of the least possible use to him. There was a great bundle of fish-hooks which Archie Phillips had bestowed upon him, more in fun than in earnest, but which Noll had treasured because Archie was his seat-mate. Then there were all sorts of relics and mementos, such as boys set their hearts upon, — bits of carved wood, favorite drawing pencils, a purple amethyst, which Johnny Moore, whose father had been in India, had given him, and, best of all, there was Ned Thorn's dear, merry face beaming upon him from out the little ebony frame in which Ned's own hands had placed it the night before his departure.

Looking at this face, and gazing upon these mementos of his friends, did not serve to make Noll at all more contented with Culm Rock and the prospect before him, and, being presently made aware of this by the heaviness which began to settle upon his heart, he closed the trunks in great haste, and ran off.

The day passed quickly enough, even for Noll, and was only the first of many happy ones spent by the shore and on the rocks. The boy had a taste for treasuring curiosities, and in the wonderful wealth of weed and shell which the sea was continually throwing upon the sand, his love of collecting and preserving was gratified. Every return of the tide was a great sweeping in of the wonders and beauties of the sea to add to his stores. There was always something new and strange to excite his delight and admiration. Then, too, there were long hours spent in climbing the rocks, till all its cliffs and hollows began to grow familiar to the boy. He climbed to Wind Cliff, and from its top looked down on the Culm houses on the sand, and into the gulls' nests far below in the crevices of the rock, and enjoyed their wild wheeling and screaming about him as he stood there. From this high look-out he often stood looking upon such sunsets as he had never seen before. High up toward the zenith the sun shot its great banners of flame as it dipped in the sea, and made the vast expanse glow and glitter. In the east the sails flitted along the purple line of the horizon, and down in the dusk shadow of the Rock he could see the grim stone house and the blue thread of smoke from Hagar's kitchen chimney. Sometimes he made use of Archie Phillips' gift, and caught fish off the rocks, much to the advantage of the old housekeeper's dinner-table.

One week after another passed, and still there seemed plenty of variety and amusement for every day. In one of his rambles, Noll came upon a little cluster of graves, with the rudest of monuments to mark them, — most of them were rough head-boards in which the sleeper's name was cut or scratched, — and this sight of such poor, uncared-for resting-places in the sand made him sad and thoughtful for more than one day. What if he were to die and be buried there, too? he surmised. The thought chilled him. True, he knew that heaven beyond was just as bright and fair for all that the graves were so forlorn and dreary; but the thought of lying far from all his friends, on bare and lonely Culm Rock, oppressed him till new sights and adventures had somewhat effaced the remembrance of the sight from his mind. Nearly one day was spent in the pine woods, whose fragrance and sombre light, and the deep hush reigning within, both awed and delighted him. Then there were days of storm and mist which could only be spent in his chamber or in the library.

Uncle Richard was generally as silent and stern as ever, and sometimes chilled the boy's heart with his coldness, and sometimes touched it by his prolonged and heavy sadness. Noll found more ways than one to make his affection known, and even when his uncle was stern almost to harshness, found some excuse for his unkindness in his warm heart, thinking that all would come right at last, and Uncle Richard lose his coldness and be as kind and regardful as he could wish. Only once did he lose his temper and rebel, and for this Noll repented heartily as soon as it was done. He went into the library one afternoon and asked permission to go around to Culm and climb up to the gulls' nests on Wind Cliff. He had explored every nook of the Rock, and this was a pleasure which he had reserved till the last, and, though not quite confident of being successful in an attempt to scale the precipitous cliff, yet he was eager and anxious enough to make the trial. Trafford was in one of his gloomiest moods, and replied, sternly, —

"You would like to break your neck, I suppose, sir, and give me the pleasure of seeing you brought home bruised and bleeding! No, you shall not go near Wind Cliff!"

The angry color came into Noll's face in an instant. "I believe it *would* be a pleasure for you to see me brought home with a broken neck!" he cried, impetuously; "and oh, I wish I were back in Hastings, where somebody cared for me!" And with this Noll hurried out of the library, slamming the door behind him.

Trafford heard these words with astonishment; then, as his nephew's footsteps died away along the hall, he covered his face and sighed heavily.

"Ah," he thought, "I did it for his good; yet—the boy distrusts me. He can't know what I would be to him if I could; how can he? He thinks me cold and unloving, and—well, he has reason to."

Hardly had ten minutes elapsed before the door swung softly open, and Noll re-entered. Trafford did not look up, did not hear him, in fact, and presently was startled by a voice saying, brokenly,—

"Uncle Richard!"

Then he looked up. Noll stood before him with downcast eyes and a trembling lip.

"Well?" said Trafford, speaking neither with coldness nor yet with kindness.

"I—I—I didn't mean what I said a few minutes ago, Uncle Richard," said Noll, chokingly; "there was not a word of truth in it, and I oughtn't to have said such a thing."

A deep silence followed, broken at last by another "Well?" from Trafford's lips.

"Will you forgive me, Uncle Richard? I was angry then, and I *don't* wish I was back at Hastings," said Noll, grieved, and fearful lest he had only put a wider gulf between himself and his uncle.

Trafford was silent so long that the boy ventured to raise his eyes. To his surprise and astonishment, his uncle was regarding him with eyes that were neither cold nor stern, but almost tender and yearning.

"Oh! do you forgive me?" Noll cried, taking hope.

Trafford laid his hand on his nephew's fair, curly hair, stroking it gently as he had once before done on the boy's arrival.

"You need not ask that, Noll," he said. "Go where you will,—I can trust you."

"But I'll not go to Wind Cliff?" said Noll, "and I wish—you don't know how much, Uncle Richard!—that I could take back those words."

"There is no need," said his uncle. "Go where you will."

Noll took his departure, more confident than ever that under Uncle Richard's coldness and seeming indifference there lurked love and regard for himself, and, true to his word, gave up all idea of ascending the cliff.

As for Trafford, though outwardly stern and cold as ever, his heart went out to the boy more yearningly after that. The month was drawing near its close, and in spite of himself, he could not regard the approaching day on which Noll's decision was to be made without some forebodings. Yet, lest the boy should be influenced by perceiving that his uncle wished his presence, Trafford was gloomier and more forbidding than ever, those last days. The boy should be perfectly free to make his choice, he thought; he would use no influence to change or bias his decision in any manner.

"Everything I have set my heart upon has been snatched away by death," he said to himself; "Noll shall stay only because it is his choice. Never will I, by look or voice, influence him to share my life and loneliness. If he stays, and I love him as my own, just so surely will death snatch him away."

But that the boy was a great comfort and delight to him he could not but confess to himself. He was surprised to find how, in those few short weeks, his cheery presence had won upon his heart. He watched him from the window as he walked on the sand below, searching for sea treasures, and could not endure the thought of having the boyish figure gone forever out of his sight. Neither could he think of the loneliness and silence which would settle down upon the old house when the gladsome voice and quick footsteps were gone, without a sigh. Now it was a great pleasure to go out to the tea-table at evening and find Noll, fresh and ruddy from his ramble on the shore and rocks, awaiting him one side the table with his grave and yet merry face. How would it be when he was gone? It were a great deal better, Trafford thought, that the boy had never come to brighten the old house with sunshine for a brief space, if now he went and left it darker and gloomier than before. And would he go? He should be left to choose for himself, the uncle thought, though the decision proved an unfavorable one.

CHAPTER VIII.

NOLL'S DECISION.

NOLL stayed. The day on which the decision was to be made he came into the library, where Trafford sat, saying, gravely, "Uncle Richard, to-day I was to choose, you know; and I would rather stay at Culm Rock and be your boy than to go back. May I?"

"May you?" exclaimed Trafford, on the impulse of the moment, while even his heavy heart was glad. "How can you ask that? Oh, Noll! do you know what you are doing?"

"To be sure, Uncle Richard! I'm going to stay with you," replied Noll, without any shadow of regret in his eyes.

"Ah, boy, I fear you will rue it," said his uncle, shaking his head mournfully; "remember, whatever befalls, that I did not bid you stay,—it was at your own risk."

"Why, what do you mean?" Noll asked, with a puzzled face,—"what is to befall me, Uncle Richard?"

"I know not,—I know not," Trafford answered; "there may be nothing to harm you; yet death ever snatches all that is dear to me, and I tremble for you, my boy."

Noll looked grave and puzzled still.

"I don't understand, Uncle Richard," he said.

"No; how can you?" his uncle said, after a pause. "To *you*, death is only God's hand; to me, it — oh, Noll, I cannot tell you what it is! I don't wish to shock you, boy, but I'm a long way from where your father was when he penned me that calm note, — lying in the very arms of death at the moment." Noll was silent. "Yes," continued Trafford, "for me there is no brightness beyond the depths of the grave. All is dark, — dark! and so many of my friends have vanished in it, — so many have been lost to me there! Ah, my hope was all wrecked long ago!"

Noll looked up quickly, with, "Papa lost to you, to me, Uncle Richard? Oh, that is not true at all! Papa *lost* to us?"

"Not to you, not to you, Noll, thank God!" Trafford replied; "but to me,—yes! His faith he left to you,—I can see, I feel it; but I have none."

Noll looked up to the sad-eyed, gloomy man, and fathomed the mystery of his sorrow at once. Who would not be forever sad with nothing beyond the grave but blank and darkness in which loved hearts were alway vanishing?

"Oh, Uncle Richard," said he, "I'm sorry for you!"

"I don't deserve it," Trafford said, with unusual tenderness. "How can you love such a man as myself? Oh, my boy, I've been harsh with you, and cold and stern; go where you'll find some one that can care for you better than I!"

But Noll's face suddenly grew bright. "I wouldn't do that," he said, earnestly,

—"never, Uncle Richard! Papa said I was to live with you and love you, and I *will*, unless you wish me to go. And if you do not, don't tell me to leave you again!"

"I will not, Noll," Trafford said.

So it was all settled at last, and Noll's heart—in spite of Uncle Richard's gloominess—was light and glad. He would stay and see if the man's sorrow and wretchedness could not be driven away, he thought; perhaps—who could tell?—he would lose his sternness, and become kind and regardful, and follow in the path which papa had trod. It all seemed very doubtful now, it was true, but such a thing *might* be, after a time.

"Yes," said Noll, as he thought of these things, "I would much rather stay with you, Uncle Richard—always. And now shall we talk about studies?"

"True, we were to consider that matter," said his uncle; "yet I had little hope that you would stay, then. What do you study, Noll?"

"At Hastings I had arithmetic and geography and Latin. Then with papa I studied history, and a little — a very little, Uncle Richard — in mineralogy, — he liked that so, you know."

"And what do you propose to do here?" asked his uncle.

"I would like to do just the same," said Noll, "and keep up with my class, perhaps."

"He has still some thoughts of returning?" Trafford wondered; then said aloud, "Well, it shall be as you like. And when will you commence?"

"At once, if you please, Uncle Richard. I've had such a long vacation that it will seem good to get back to books once more; they're all waiting for me up-stairs. Shall I get them?"

Noll bounded away as his uncle nodded assent, and went up-stairs with a merry whistle. Trafford listened to the quick footsteps and the light-hearted music, and really rejoiced that they were not to flee and leave the old house desolate. It would be a brighter dwelling than it had been till—till death came, he thought. And if he could not teach the boy as Brother Noll had desired him to do, yet he would see that in the matter of books and study he had every advantage. So, when the boy came down with his arms full of books, he set himself to his task with an earnestness that pleased Noll wonderfully.

"Uncle Richard means that I shall progress," he thought; "and oh, I *do* hope I can keep up with Ned and the rest!"

Trafford found his nephew an apt scholar. He had expected that, however, for the boy came of a book-loving race. Very likely, had the pupil proved but a dull one, he would sometimes have wearied of his task of hearing the recitations every day; but as it was, he found a positive pleasure in his capacity as Noll's instructor, and generally a relief from his gloominess.

Noll's study-hours were at his own discretion; the recitations came in the afternoon, and after four the boy had the remainder of the day to spend as he liked. Sometimes the shore claimed him, sometimes the rocks. Then there were excursions, in company with old Hagar, to the solitude of the pines, after cones and dry, resinous branches for the kitchen fire, which never seemed to burn well unless the old housekeeper had an abundance of this kindling material.

"Nuffin like dem yer pine cones fur winter mornin's," Hagar always said; and many were the visits which she and "Mas'r Noll" paid to the woods, returning with laden baskets.

Somehow, after a time, the boy found more delight in these simple pleasures than at first. Once, with all his friends about him, he would have found no entertainment in a journey into the forest after cones,— there were other delights in abundance, then; but now, forced to get all his enjoyment out of the simplest, humblest events, this work of gathering winter fuel grew to be a positive pleasure, after the recitations were over, and the short

October days drawing to a close. Then, too, the winter stores were being brought down from Hastings on the "Gull," and Skipper Ben and his crew came often to the stone house, to break the monotony of days in some little manner.

"Yer 'live an' hearty yet, lad!" was his greeting as he came around in the "Gull's" boat with a variety of provisions for winter use, one cloudy afternoon. "Well, I mus' say I didn't think to find ye so? Lonesome any? Goin' to let me carry ye back to Hastings afore the 'Gull' stops runnin'?"

"No," said Noll, bravely, "I'm going to stay, skipper."

"Ye'll find the weather a tough un, bime-by," drawled Mr. Snape, as he rolled a flour-barrel up the sand.

"Yes," said the skipper, "winters are

mos'ly hard uns down here. An' what ye goin' to do when the 'Gull' stops cruisin' fur the season, an' ye can't get a word frum the city?"

This was a contingency for which Noll had made no calculation. Not hear a word from Hastings for a whole long winter?

"Well," he said at last, "that isn't pleasant to think of, but I'll manage somehow, skipper. And you must bring me a great packet of letters to last till the 'Gull' commences her trips again."

"Ay, lad," said the skipper, his eyes twinkling. "What be these?" drawing a parcel from under his pea-jacket.

Noll's eager "Letters! and for me?" tickled the old sailor wonderfully.

"Yes, these be letters," he said, chuckling; "Jack, here, talks o' runnin' a smack down this winter purpose to bring yer mail!"

"'Tw'u'd take something bigger'n a smack," observed Mr. Snape, looking askance to see how Noll grasped the precious parcel.

"All yer frien's said as how I was to bring ye back on the 'Gull,'" called the skipper after him, as Noll went running across the sand toward the house.

"Oh, how I wish — No! I can't go, skipper; it's no use talking," Noll answered back as he gained the piazza, and there sat down to open his precious missives.

Five or six of his boy friends had agreed to surprise him each with a letter, and here they were, together with a kind note from Mr. Gray. What a comfort and pleasure they were! It was almost like seeing the writers' faces and talking with them, Noll thought.

Trafford came out upon the piazza while he sat there absorbed in their contents, and as he walked along toward the skipper, who stood waiting at the bottom of the steps, noted the boy's eager, delighted face, and wondered why the lad did not return to his friends, where, it was quite evident, he was much desired and longed for. Why did he stay on this dreary Rock? What was there here to make the place endurable for a boy of his age and tastes? He could not see.

Those were the last letters which Noll received. The "Gull" made one or two trips after that, but the first of November brought keen, sleety weather, and Skipper Ben came no more; so that for the long months ahead Culm Rock was to be shut out from the world entirely. The thought of being isolated from all assistance, in case of illness or trouble, oppressed Noll somewhat till he had accustomed himself to the thought, and then a vague dread of loneliness and homesickness in the dragging days of winter haunted him for a time. But getting bravely over these, and interested in his studies, he began to find that the November days were not so intolerable, after all.

Uncle Richard had surprised him one day by bringing in a writing-table, from one of the unoccupied rooms, and placing it opposite his own chair by one of the tall windows. "For your books, Noll," he had said; and from thenceforth the boy's well-worn school volumes had a place there, and study in the cold chamber was exchanged for the comfortable warmth of the library. It was not an unpleasant schoolroom, by any means, though the high, old window framed nothing but a great stretch of sea and sky, — both, this chilly month of November, often gray and misty.

Instead of the roar and din of the city which sounded about the dearly-remembered room at Hastings, there was the hoarse murmur of the tide on its rocks and pebbles, the wild whirling of the wind and its screaming around the corners and over the chimney, — not cheery sounds, any of them; yet, in the still afternoons, and the cozy quietness of long evenings when the lamp shed its mild light over the room, and the fire on the hearth shone redly, there was such calm and peace for books and study as Noll found both pleasant and profitable.

In these days, you may be sure, the boy's thoughts were often across the vast gray sea in front of his window, even when he was bending over his problems or translations; not that he regretted his decision to share Uncle Richard's life with him, nor that he had any thoughts of fleeing away, but those flitting sails on the far horizon were messengers which alway bore on their white wings thoughts of hope and love and patience to those over the sea.

It was not the natural sphere of a boy, — this monotonous, unvarying round of days, with no companions of his age or tastes; and, as week after week passed, and Noll was still blithe and apparently contented, Trafford wondered and conjectured, and could not surmise a reason for it; though, had he observed closely, it would not have been a great mystery. For Noll there was the unfailing comfort of the little Bible which lay beside the huge old bed up-stairs, and which gave the double comfort of its own blessedness and the remembrance of its preciousness to her who turned its pages to the last; and there were ever the pitying ears of Jesus ready to hear the story of discouragement and loneliness, when the burden of slow, weary days seemed *too* heavy to bear.

Into Trafford's life had come more brightness and content than he had known since that dark day when his wife left him and vanished in the darkness which, to his eyes, filled and hovered over the grave. It did not, as yet, seem like a real and lasting joy; he trembled lest some day it should prove but a dream, a vision, and so vanish. He often laid aside his book and looked up, half expecting to find the room as silent and lonely as when, of old, he was the only inhabitant of the great library; but there, at the opposite window, sat the pleasant figure of the boy, busy with his books, and as real and tangible as heart could wish. It was a perpetual delight, though he hid all knowledge of it from Noll, to feel that the boy was present, to see him curled up in a great chair by the fire, watching the flames or the depths of rosy coal, of a twilight, and to feel that he was *his*,—a precious gift to love and cherish. So the man's heart began to go out toward the boy,—tremblingly, warningly at first, then, as he found him true and worthy, with all its might and all the fervor of which it was capable.

CHAPTER IX.

DIRK'S TROUBLE.

NOLL closed his books one afternoon after recitations, saying, "I'll put on my overcoat, Uncle Richard, and take a run up the shore, — just for exercise. The waves are monstrous, and how they thunder! I haven't seen them so large since I came to Culm."

"Look out for the tide," continued his

uncle; "keep away from that narrow strip of sand up the shore, for the waves will cover it in an hour."

Noll promised to be cautious, and ran off after cap and overcoat. Hagar met him as he came down from his room all muffled for the walk, and exclaimed,—

"Bress ye, honey! where ye bound fur now? Dis yer is a dreffful bad time on de shore! I's 'feard to hev ye roun' dar!" looking at him anxiously.

Noll laughed merrily. "Do you think I'm too small to take care of myself, Hagar?" he asked; "I'm only going for a walk, and to see the waves. I'll be back for supper with Uncle Richard."

The sky was wild and gray with clouds. A keen, chilly wind swept fiercely over the rocks and along the shore, and the dark, foam-fringed waves rode grandly in upon the beach with a thunderous shock as they flew into spray. Some of the spray mist wet Noll's face, even as he stood upon the piazza steps. But, warmly clad, and loving the sight of the wild tumult, he started with a light heart for his walk up the shore. As far as he could see, the sea was dark and gloomy, with long curves of foam whitening its surface and gleaming on the crests of its racing waves. At his feet, on the sand, lay great tangles of kelp and flecks of yeasty froth. The air was keen, and frosty enough to film the still pools in the hollows with brittle ice, and where the spray fell upon the rocks, it congealed and cased the old boulders with glittering mail. Not a sail was there in sight, and Noll thought the sea had never looked so vast and lonely as now. Along the horizon the clouds were white-edged, and seemed to open and lead away into illimitable distances of vapor. He stopped under the shelter of a rock to look behind him, over the path which he had trodden. The stone house looked dark and forbidding, like everything else under this wild gray sky; but Noll had long ago ceased to consider it as resembling a prison. It was home, now, and so took a fairer, brighter shape in his eyes. Beyond, the pines stood up against the sky, full of sombreness and inky shadow.

"How cold and desolate everything is!" thought Noll; "but it's not half so gloomy as it seems, after all. I wish, though, that Ned — dear fellow! — was here, just to make it lively once in a while." He walked on, listening to the heavy thunder of waves, and looking upon the troubled waste of sea, till he came to the curve of the shore. Here lay the narrow path of pebbles against which his uncle had warned him. But there seemed no immediate danger, for the path looked as wide as ever, and as there was yet an hour before the tide would be in, Noll hurried across, the salt spray flying wildly about him.

"I'll go on a little further," he thought, "and I shall get home long enough before tea-time, then."

Having gone a little way, however, he chanced to remember that he had not been at Culm village for a month, at least, and longed to take a run down to the little cluster of houses.

"How the waves will dash in there!" he thought; "and I wonder how those huts stand such a tempest as this? I've a good mind to go, anyhow, — it's such a good chance to see the place in a gale." He wavered and walked hesitatingly about in the sand for a few minutes, and at last decided to go. He ran and walked by turns, the wind blowing his curly locks in his eyes and taking his breath almost away with its fierce gusts; yet he kept on. It seemed as if the waves jarred and thundered heavier on this Culm side than on his own quarter of the Rock; at any rate, the wind was more powerful, and blew the spray upon him in showers.

"I'll get drenched, if the wind keeps on like this!" he thought; "if I weren't so near, I'd turn back; but the houses are in sight, already, and I've got to get acquainted with salt water. I'll keep on!"

When he drew near the little settlement, he was tired enough with running and battling the wind, and was content to take a slower pace. Never had the fishermen's huts looked so forlorn and miserable as now. Noll half expected to see them come tumbling and rolling along the sand in every gust of wind which struck them; yet, with some mysterious attraction to their sandy foundations, they held their own, though some of them creaked and groaned with the strain which was brought to bear upon their timbers.

The boy kept on toward the little wharf, over which the waves rolled and tumbled furiously, without meeting a soul. The water dashed so high and wildly up the sand that he was obliged to keep well up beside the houses to escape a drenching. He thought he had never looked upon so grand a sight as the sea presented here,

— all its vast waste lashed into great waves that came roaring in like white-maned monsters to dash themselves upon the land.

Standing here, close by Dirk Sharp's door, Noll suddenly fancied he heard a faint wail within. He was not at all sure, the sea thundered so, and the wind screamed so shrilly about the miserable dwelling; but presently, in a slight lull of the tempest, he heard the wail — if wail it was — again. It sounded like the voice of a child, — a child suffering illness or pain.

"I wonder if Dirk has any little ones?" thought Noll; "and what can he do with them, if they are ill?"

Mentally hoping that his ears had deceived him, and that no one on the desolate Rock stood in need of aid which they could not have, he was about to turn away and retrace his steps homeward, as the sky seemed to shut down grayer and darker than before, and nightfall was approaching. But at that instant the door of the dwelling opened, and out came Dirk, beating his breast and crying aloud, whether with pain or grief Noll was too surprised to notice at first.

The man failed to see the lad standing close by his door-step till he had taken several strides up and down the sand, where the wind blew the spray full upon him, — walking there hatless and coatless. When he did perceive him, he stopped short, exclaiming, almost fiercely, —

"What *ye* here fur, lad? — what ye here fur? The Lord knows it's no place fur the sort ye b'long to!"

"I was looking at the sea," said Noll; "and — and — what's the matter, Dirk?"

"Nothin' that'll do ye any good ter know!" cried Dirk, roughly, beginning to pace up and down the sand again. "Ye can't know nothin' o' trouble, lad! How ken ye?"

Noll hardly knew what answer to make to this vehement question, and finally made none at all, but asked, —

"Are any of your family ill, Dirk?"

"Ill? Sick, ye mean? O Lord! yes, yes, — and dyin'!"

Noll started. Some one ill and dying on this dreary, wretched Rock! and no doctor to give aid. He did not know how far he might dare to interrogate Dirk in his present half-frenzied condition, but ventured, after a minute or two of silence, to ask, —

"Is it one of the children?"

"Yes, my little gal!" said Dirk, groaning, — "my little gal it is, an' nothin' to keep her frum it. O Lord! seems as ef I sh'u'd go mad!" and he threw up his hands to the lowering sky in despair, and faced about to the sea, letting the cold drops drive into his face.

Noll was fain to comfort him, but was at a loss how to offer consolation to such anguish as Dirk's.

"Isn't there some one on the Rock that can help, that knows something about medicine?" he asked, eagerly.

"No, no, lad!" Dirk cried, "there ain't a soul this side o' the sea ken help my little gal! Ye don' know nothin' o' trouble, lad! Ye don' know what 'tis ter feel that yer chile's dyin' fur want o' somethin' to save it! O Lord! seems as ef I c'u'd swim through this sea to Hastings fur my little gal!"

He rushed down to the boiling surf, and Noll half expected to see him throw himself into the sea; but he came back, drenched with a great wave, with dèspair and agony upon his face.

"Here, lad," he exclaimed, "come in,—come in an' see what trouble is! Ye don' know. How ken ye?"

Noll followed, and Dirk pushed open the door of his dwelling. The air which met the boy as he entered the small, low room was so close and foul that he almost staggered back. The floor was bare, and through a crack under the door the keen wind swept in across it, flaring the fire on the stone hearth and puffing ashes and smoke about. A fishy odor was upon everything. Household utensils were scattered about in front of the hearth, occupying a quarter of the room, and what few chairs and other articles of wooden furniture there were, were fairly black with dirt and smoke. Noll had never before entered a dwelling so filthy, wretched, and miserable as this.

"Here, lad," said Dirk, brokenly,—"here—be—the—little gal," and pointed to one corner, where, watched over by a thin, slovenly woman, the child lay on its little bed.

The mother did not take her eyes off the girl, and Noll went forward, with much inward repugnance, to look upon Dirk's treasure. The child's cheeks were flushed a bright red, and it lay with drowsy, heavy-lidded eyes, uttering, at intervals, a low wail.

Noll shivered, and involuntarily thought of those dreary, desolate graves which he stumbled upon in one of his rambles.

Could nothing be done? Must the child die for lack of a little medicine? He looked through the little dirt-crusted window upon the tossing sea, and saw what a hopeless barrier it interposed between them and aid. He thought of Uncle Richard, and knew that it was useless to expect aid from that direction; and then he thought of *Hagar!* She was a good nurse, he remembered, and knew — or claimed to know — a vast deal about medicine. Perhaps she could help this child! he thought, with a glad heart, and if she could! His heart suddenly sank, for he remembered that the old housekeeper could not make a journey through the storm and tempest, even had she the necessary skill.

"But," he thought to himself, "I can tell her about the child, — it's got a fever, —

and she can send medicines; and to-morrow, if it's pleasant, she can come herself!" and thinking thus, Noll turned to Dirk, with—

"I can get you some medicines, I think, from our old housekeeper. May I? Shall I try?"

The fisherman was silent with surprise. He would probably have sooner expected aid from across the raging sea than from this lad.

Noll read an answer in his eyes, and hastened to the door, and bounded away without waiting for any more words or explanations.

How fast it had grown dark while he was in Dirk's hut! The horizon was quite hidden, so was all the wide waste a half-mile from shore; but with the coming of night the sea had lost none of its thunder, nor the wind aught of its fierceness. Noll ran till he was out of breath. Then he walked, thinking that the homeward path was wonderfully long. Then he ran again, feeling almost as if the child's life depended upon his exertions, and seeming to hear its wail above all the din of wind and waves.

Suddenly he plashed into the water, up to his ankles, and this brought his headlong race to an abrupt termination. What could it mean? Then he remembered, with a sudden chill, what, in his eagerness and anxiety, he had entirely forgotten, — the tide was coming in, and was already over the path which Uncle Richard warned him against.

He looked back. The beach over which he had come glimmered faintly in the dusk, with its long line of breakers gleaming far up and down. Back there in the darkness, he thought, Dirk's child was dying for want of medicine. Oh! what to do? He looked down at the foam creeping about his ankles, and said to himself, —

"Pshaw! it's only over shoe, now, and my feet are wet already. I'll dash through; 'twon't take but three minutes, and I *can't* wait!"

He sprang on, thinking to clear the short strip, which the tide had covered, with a few bounds. A wave, high and broad, which had been gathering power and volume in all its long, onward course, came sweeping thunderingly in and engulfed him.

CHAPTER X.

IN THE SEA.

NOLL'S presence of mind enabled him to clutch the jagged sides of the rock desperately, so that in the wave's return he was not drawn with it into the sea depths. Stunned, strangled, half blinded, and impelled by a sudden horror of death in the cold, treacherous sea, he took two or three forward steps, fell, then rose and strove to struggle on. But a little hollow in the path let him down into the flood to his waist. The spray flew into his eyes and mouth, and breathless and bewildered he fell again, this time to disappear under the foam-flecked water. He struggled up to air and life at last, with many gasps for breath, and once more clutched at the rocks behind him. It all seemed like the terror of a dream, not real and threatening. Was he to be drowned? Some sudden thought of the pleasantness of life, of dear friends across this same cruel, ravenous sea, of Uncle Richard and his warning, came to him here. To be drowned in this dark, chill, raging flood? Oh! no, no! Then he saw, out in the gloom and mistiness, the white gleaming of a wave-crest, rising and sinking, but sweeping steadily toward him, and knew that it would dash upon his narrow foothold. Could he survive another?

Then from Noll's lips came a shrill cry, which rose above the thunder and battering of the sea; and, whether from terror or whether from the fact that the dear name was so warm and vivid in his heart at that moment, the cry was not "Help!" but, "Papa, papa!"

The cry was answered!—at least, Noll fancied it was, and clung to the jagged edges of rock with a new love of life in his heart, and, with his eyes on the approaching wave, which began to loom up dark and vast, cried out again with all his might.

Out of the darkness which hovered over his submerged path beyond, a figure came struggling, — battling the water and making desperate efforts to run, — crying, —

"Noll, Noll! where are you?"

"Here, — Uncle Richard, — quick!" answered the boy, clinging desperately to his only refuge, — the slippery, icy rocks.

The wave came thunderingly in, burst, and hid uncle and nephew from each other. Trafford uttered a groan of despair, and stood, for an instant, like one palsied. Back swept the flood, leaving the sand bare for a minute, and with a shout, the master of the stone house rushed forward, seized the figure which had fallen there, and sprang away toward the sand and safety. He gained it, and tremblingly laid his burden down. Had he only saved a body from which the life had flown?

"Oh, Noll!" he cried, brokenly, — "Noll, Noll!"

Only the sea and the wailing of the

wind answered him. Hurriedly gathering the boy in his arms, he started for the house, running and stumbling through the sand and over the rocks, fearful lest he should reach its warmth and shelter too late. But before he had gained half the distance between him and the redly-gleaming window, where he knew Hagar was sitting before her fire, Noll stirred in his arms. Trafford stopped, fearing that his excited imagination had deceived him.

"Noll," he cried, "speak to me,—speak!"

"Yes—only—I'm—I'm so cold," chattered Noll, faintly; "and—Uncle Richard—you—you've saved me!"

Trafford could not speak, so great was the load which had suddenly lifted from his heart. He started on with his burden, though Noll protested against being carried, and at every step rejoiced within himself. What cared he for the thunder of the sea, the wind's screaming, and the terror of death which they boded? *His* treasure was safe, safe!—torn from the very yawning mouth of the deep, and what were wreck and disaster of others to him? He came to the little kitchen, presently, the light from its one window toward the shore beaming cheerily upon him, and threw open the door and entered so suddenly that Hagar screamed out with affright.

"De good Lord help us now!" she cried at the sight of the master and his burden. "What's happened, Mas'r Dick?"

Noll answered, assuringly, "Nothing very serious, Hagar. I've been in—the sea. Oh, Uncle Richard! how did you find me?"

Trafford set his burden down upon the

three-legged stool which Hagar had just vacated, saying,—

"I was looking for you, Noll, and heard your cry. O Heaven! what if I had failed to hear it!"

"I should have been swept away," said Noll.

Here Hagar recovered her wits sufficiently to give a little howl of lamentation.

"Out ob de sea! out ob de sea!" she cried; "de Lord be t'anked fur it! Dat yer sea am a dreffful t'ing, honey,—allers swallerin', swallerin', an' nebber ken get 'nough fur itself, nohow. Hagar's seen it; she knows what dat yer sea is, an' t'ank de Lord, he's let ye come out of it alive. Mas'r Dick, why don't ye t'ank Him fur savin' ob yer boy fur ye?"

"Hush!" said Trafford, his face growing gloomy; "find Noll some dry clothes, Hagar. Quick, woman!"

"Yes, in a minnit, Mas'r Dick; quick's I ken git dis yer ole candle lit. But ef ye don't t'ank de Lord now, ye'll have to come to it 'fore long, Mas'r Dick; Hagar tells ye so! dat yer time'll come! it'll come!"

"Hush!" said Trafford, harshly, "and do as I bade you."

Hagar went out, sighing, "Dat time'll come, dat time'll come, bress de Lord!"

Noll looked up from his seat by the fire, where he sat dripping and shivering, and said, —

"But aren't you glad I'm safe, Uncle Richard?—aren't you thankful?"

Trafford answered this question with a look which made his nephew exclaim, —

"I know you are, Uncle Richard! Then why — why — aren't you thankful to God?"

"Don't, don't, Noll!" said his uncle.

"Strip off those wet garments and make haste to get warm again. Culm Rock is no place for one to be sick in. Hurry, boy?"

Instead of hurrying, however, Noll suddenly grew very grave and exclaimed,—

"Oh, I've forgotten something, Uncle Richard! That tide drove it all out of my head. What can I do? Dirk Sharp's little girl is sick—dying, and I was to bring her some medicine, if Hagar had any!"

"What is Dirk or his to you?" exclaimed Trafford. "Was that what kept you so late? Is that how you came to be caught by the tide?"

"Yes," said Noll, "I—"

His uncle interrupted him with a stern, "Noll, you reckless lad! What are those Culm people to us,—to me? You put your life in peril — oh, I tremble to think *what* peril! — for Dirk's miserable child? What were you thinking of? Have you no regard for your life, — for my happiness?"

"Why," said Noll, quickly, "Dirk loves his child as well as you love me, and I thought perhaps Hagar's medicines could help it, and I didn't know there was any peril till I got into it; and oh, Uncle Richard, what will they do now that I can't come back?"

"I don't know," said Trafford, gloomily; "they are accustomed to such things, I suppose. Shall I have to command you to take off those wet clothes?"

Noll began to remove his ice-cold garments, but presently said, —

"Is there, — do you think there'll be any hope of my going back to-night, Uncle Richard? The child is dreadful sick, you know."

"Going back!—to-night! Are you crazy, Noll?" Trafford cried. "No, you will not put foot outside the door this night!"

"But, Un—"

"Hush! not another word," said his uncle, sternly. "If you have no regard for your life, I must have for you. Hagar is waiting at the door with your dry clothes. Are you ready for them?"

Noll answered "Yes," his heart suddenly filled with a dreary recollection of the sight which he had seen in Dirk's miserable abode. It seemed to him as if he could hear the sick child's wail above the war of the storm. Dirk, he thought, would watch and wait for his return, peering through the dirty little window into the gathering gloom and darkness, and, finding that he did not come, would settle back into despair again.

Noll put on the dry garments with a heavy heart. He was sure he felt strong enough to return to Culm, and although the sea barred the beach path, yet, with a lantern, he could find a way over the rocks, he thought. But Uncle Richard had utterly refused; so there was no hope, and the child must suffer on, and Dirk watch in vain.

"Oh," thought Noll, "why wasn't I more careful? Why *didn't* I think of the tide? Then nothing would have happened, and I could have gone back!"

Hagar came in, saying, "Ye'll hab yer supper here, in de kitchen, Mas'r Noll, 'cause it's warmer fur ye dan in de dinin'-room. Ye won't mind Hagar's ole kitchen jes' fur once, honey?"

"No," said Noll, sadly, "I won't mind at all, Hagar, and I'm not hungry—much."

Trafford went out to change his own wet clothing. The old housekeeper bustled between her cupboards and a little round table which she had drawn before the fire, casting wistful looks at Noll as he sat gravely gazing in the coals.

"Bress de Lord! bress de Lord fur savin' ye!" she ejaculated, fervently, as she bent down over her tea-pot which was spouting odorous jets of steam from its place on the hearth; "'pears like dar wouldn't be nuffin left in dis ole house ef de sea had swallered ye, Mas'r Noll. Don't *ye* t'ank de Lord?" she asked, peering up into the boy's sober face.

"Yes; I'm glad to live, and I thank God for saving me; but oh, Hagar," said Noll, almost with tears in his eyes, "there's somebody on this Rock to-night that's as sad as you or Uncle Richard would have been if the tide had swept me away!"

"Now!" said Hagar; "an' who is dem yer?"

"Dirk Sharp's little girl is sick with a fever, and I think she's going to die,—though of course I can't tell,—and they haven't a drop of medicine. Just think, Hagar,—dying, and nothing to save!"

Hagar thought, and sighed heavily over her tea-pot. "Don' know what's goin' to 'come o' them yer Culm folks!" she said.

"And," continued Noll, "I promised to bring Dirk some medicine,—I was going to get it of you; but I got into that fearful tide and was half drowned, and now—oh, what can I do?"

"Bress ye, honey, ye didn't 'spect to go back in de dark to Culm?" cried Hagar.

"I would—if Uncle Richard hadn't forbidden," said Noll; "do you think you have any medicines that can help the child, Hagar?"

"Don' know," shaking her turbaned head. "Ef 'twas rheumatiz, or ef 'twas a cut, or ef 'twas one o' dem yer colds, Hagar'd 'spect to know; but can't tell nuffin 'bout fevers, nohow. 'Tw'u'd be jes' as de Lord's willin'!"

"Will you go, or send something in the morning?" queried Noll.

"Ef it's pleasant, honey, Hagar'll go wid ye. Yer supper's waiting fur ye!"

Noll sighed, and did not stir. The misery which he had seen in Dirk's wretched hut haunted him.

Hagar poured out the boy's cup of tea, waited a little space, then returned it to its steaming pot again.

"Come, yer supper's cold 'nough, now, honey," said she, coming up to Noll's seat. "What ye waitin' fur? Oh, chile, ye grows more'n' more like yer poor father. T'inkin' ob de mis'ry ober dar; ain't ye?"

"*Such* misery, too!" said Noll.

"Well, dar's mis'ry eberywhere!" said Hagar; "can't go nowhere but what ye'll find it. Yer Uncle Dick has had mis'ry 'nough in his day, but 'tain't done him no good 'tall. Jes' froze his heart up harder'n a stone."

"It isn't all stone," said Noll.

"Don' ye t'ink so? Well, 'pears like ye's sent here by de Lord, jes' to break dat heart ob his all to pieces!" said Hagar, earnestly.

"Sent here to break Uncle Richard's heart?" laughed Noll. "Well, I wonder if he thinks I came here for that purpose?"

"Don' know," said the old housekeeper, with a shake of her head; "but dat's what I t'ink de Lord sent ye here fur. Dat heart ob his is all frizzed up. 'Spects 'twon't be so allus, chile, — de Lord helpin'."

Noll ate his supper, bade Hagar good-night, admonishing her to "be sure and have the medicines ready the first thing!" and groped his way to the library, where his uncle was sitting at his organ.

Trafford stopped playing the instant the door opened, and as Noll drew near, put his arm about him, saying,—

"My boy!—*mine!*—doubly my own since I snatched you from death! Oh, Noll! if I had lost you!"

The boy sighed. "Dirk has got to lose *his* child," he said, "and oh, Uncle Richard, I should be a great deal happier if I might only try to save it!"

"Hush!" said his uncle; "do you think I would let you go forth on such a night? Never, never! Death is always near, Noll, and you cannot know what a blow it would be to me should it grasp you! No, you shall stay and be safe."

In Noll's fervent prayer that night there was pleading for Uncle Richard as well as thanks for the mercy which saved him from the drowning sea.

CHAPTER XI.

DIRK'S TREASURE.

AT the first gray glimmer of the wintry dawn, Noll was awake. He felt stiff and lame after his adventure of the previous evening, and not at all inclined to stir. But a sudden recollection of Dirk and his child, and the aid which he had promised them, came to him almost as soon as he was conscious of the day's dawning, and he got up and limped to the window to see whether there was any prospect of Hagar's journey to Culm being realized. The sky was as gray and sombre as yesterday's had been. All the sea was in a great turmoil, and rolled in a flood of foam upon the shore as far as he could see. Not a sail in sight upon the lonely waste, not a sign of human life anywhere. Now and then a snow-flake fluttered down; and the wind screamed shrilly about the house-corners, and wailed hoarsely in the casements.

"Hagar can't go to-day," thought Noll, with a sinking heart; "and, oh! what *can* be done?"

He trembled for fear Uncle Richard would forbid him to go to Culm again. He felt as if he could never bear to meet Dirk's eyes after promising him aid and failing to bring it; and, with this thought oppressing him, and the lonely cry of the sea filling his ears, he dressed himself, and went down to the library with a downcast heart. His uncle sat by a window, looking, with a sad and gloomy face, upon the sea; and, as his nephew entered, acknowledged his "Good-morning, Uncle Richard," with only a cold nod. But Noll, resolved to have the matter settled at once, came up to his chair, saying, —

"I've got a great favor to ask of you, Uncle Richard. May I go around to Culm after breakfast?"

Trafford's face grew gloomier than before.

"For what?" he asked.

"To carry something for Dirk's child," Noll answered, meeting his uncle's stern eyes with his own pleading blue ones.

"Pshaw!" exclaimed Trafford, impatiently, "what are these miserable fish-folks to you? I don't want you to care for them!"

"But, Uncle Richard—"

"Well?"

"Dirk's child is sick,—dying, I'm afraid!"

"So are hundreds in this world. There's misery everywhere."

"Perhaps I might aid this misery, Uncle Richard, if you'll let me try. Will you?"

"You will have more than your hands full if you are going to look after these Culm people," said Trafford, coldly; "you had better not begin."

Noll's face grew graver and graver, and he made no reply to his uncle's last remark.

"Well," said Trafford, after a long silence, "do you wish anything more, Noll?"

The boy turned away, as if hurt by his uncle's coldness, and walked quickly to the library door. There he wavered — stopped — then turned about, and came back.

"Uncle Richard," said he, tremulously, "papa said I was to do all the good I could in the world, and never pass by any trouble that I might help, and — and I think he would tell me to go to Dirk's, if he were here."

Trafford turned about with an impatient word upon his lips, but it was not spoken. It seemed to him as if his dead brother stood before him, — as he had known him when they were boys together, — and that those words were meant for a reproach. He put out his hand and touched Noll's shoulder, as if to make sure that it was really his nephew and no vision.

"Ah!" said he, with a sigh, "your father looks out at me from your eyes, Noll. Turn them away from me. Go to

Culm, if you like, — you have my permission."

"Breakfas's waitin' fur ye!" said Hagar, at the door.

"But, Uncle Richard," said Noll, in some perplexity, "I don't like to go and have you all the time wishing me at home."

"I cannot help that," said Trafford, as he rose to answer Hagar's call. "I have given you permission, — go."

The breakfast was a silent one. After it was over, and the door had closed upon the grim master of the house as he went back to his books, Hagar said, —

"Don't ye let nuffin make ye down-hearted, honey! De Lord'll help ye, ef yer Uncle Dick won't. 'Tain't de might nor de money dat'll do eberyting, chile. All 'pends on whether de Lord's on yer

"Dis yer is brof." Page 183.

side. Jes' come in my ole kitchen and see what I's put up fur ye to carry to dem yer mis'able folks."

Noll got his overcoat and cap, and followed the old housekeeper into her cozy and comfortable dominion.

"Look at dis yer," said Hagar, taking a basket off the table; "jes' as chock full as nuffin ye ken think ob. Dis yer is brof, — chicken-brof, — an' dat yer bundle is crackers. Dis bottle's de med'cine, an' de chile is to hab a teaspoonful ebery half an hour. Ef I could be there, de chile should hab a sweat, sure; but dis med'cine'll hev to answer! Dis yer is a teaspoon an' a teacup, 'cause ye won't find nuffin fit fur to drink nuffin out ob. Hagar knows how dem yer Culm folks lib! Now, ken ye 'member all dat, honey?"

"Yes," said Noll, "and I thank you a

hundred times, Hagar. I'd better start at once, without waiting another minute."

The old housekeeper followed him to the door, cautioning, "Keep 'way from dat yer sea, chile! Don't yer git into dat yer drefful tide, honey! an' de Lord bress ye an' bring ye safe back!"

The wind was keen and bitter, and the sea thundered as mightily as on the previous evening. Noll hurried along over the great patches of icy sea-weed and frozen pools of water in the rocks and hollows, and thought, now that he was making such haste, that the way had never seemed quite so long before. He paused for a moment to look upon the scene of last night's peril, and remember, with a shudder, how the waves battered, and how they pierced and numbed him with their cold. Then he ran along the hard, sandy beach as fast as the wind and his burden would let him. The Culm huts came in sight at last, cheerless and desolate, and with no sign of life or occupancy about them, save the faint smoke which the wind whirled down from the chimneys.

Noll began to regard Dirk's habitation with anxious eyes long before he drew near. He half expected to see the fisherman's tall figure pacing up and down the sand, beating his breast and groaning with despair, perhaps; but instead, the sands were deserted. Noll came opposite the miserable dwelling, and paused a few seconds before rapping, waiting to hear the sick child's low wail. He heard only a confused, unintelligible murmur of voices.

A woman answered his summons,—not the child's mother, but a neighbor, evidently,—and stood staring blankly at him.

"Can I see Dirk,—Dirk Sharp?" Noll asked.

At the sound of the boy's voice, the fisherman himself came to the door. His face was haggard, and looked wan and worn, for all the bronze of wind and weather that was upon it.

"Lord bless ye, lad!" he cried to Noll, "but ye be too late."

"Too late?"

"Yes," brokenly, "my little gal died las' night."

Noll was silent with surprise. He was too late,—too late.

"Oh, Dirk," he said, as soon as he could speak, "I would have come back last night, but I got into the sea, and—and it was impossible. So I brought what I could this morning."

Dirk looked at the lad and his basket,

and choked. At last he said, gratefully, "It be good in ye to care for the like o' us, lad. We be poor folks fur ye to look at, the Lord knows! What did ye bring fur my little gal?"

Noll lifted the cover of his basket, and Dirk peered in, exclaiming, "My little gal never seed the like o' them, lad! She wur a tender thing, my little gal wur, and mabby ef she'd had a bit o' somethin' better'n the salt fish — Well, she be beyond meat and drink now," he said, choking again.

Noll knew not whether to turn back, or to stay. Dirk, however, presently said, "Come, lad, step in an' see my little gal. She wur as white an' sof'-cheeked as yerself. O Lord! I might ha' knowed she'd never come up stout an' growin' like the rest," he groaned as he turned back to lead the way for Noll.

In the room where the little one had lain sat three or four old fish-wives,—wrinkled, weather-beaten old faces they had,—who were nodding and whispering over their pipes in a solemn kind of way, occasionally addressing a word to the mother, who sat enveloped in the smoke which poured into the room from the ill-constructed fireplace. They regarded Noll with many curious glances as he passed through after Dirk to the apartment where the child was laid, and one old creature followed after them, apparently to ascertain the boy's errand.

It was a bare room where Dirk's treasure was sleeping,—not a thing in it save the two wooden stools and rough board which upheld their still little burden. Pure and white the child lay,—a fair, delicate flower when compared with the dinginess and squalor of everything about it; and something of this contrast seemed to glimmer upon Dirk's rough perceptions, for he said to Noll,—

"Ye wouldn't think she could be mine, lad! Ye don't wonder the little gal couldn't come up like the rest o' the young uns?"

"It wur a fair gal, Lord knows," said the old fish-wife who had followed them in; "it warn't black and freckly, never. Sich kinds don't love this salt water, Dirk Sharp,—ye couldn't ha' raised her, man!"

"Oh, my little gal!" murmured Dirk, smoothing a fleck of golden hair with his great brawny hand.

"Ye be fair an' white," said the old fish-wife, touching Noll's cheek with her skinny finger, "an' what be ye here on the Rock fur?"

"Sh!—ye let the lad alone, mother," said Dirk; "he be come here to bring my little gal somethin', an' she be beyond eatin' an' drinkin'. He be a good lad to do it!"

Noll looked upon the little sleeper's face, and then at the wretched surroundings, and was glad for the child's sake that sleep and peace had come at last. Yet his heart was heavy as he looked upon his basket and its now useless contents, and he thought, "Oh, if I had only been more careful last night!—perhaps—perhaps Hagar's medicines could have helped it." He turned to Dirk, saying, quietly,—

"I must go now. I'm—I'm *so* sorry I was too late!"

The fisherman followed Noll out on to the sand, and, as the boy was about to turn away homeward, took both his hands in one of his own great brown ones, saying,—

"Ye be kinder to me 'an I ken tell ye, lad. I thought yer kind had no heart fur us folk. Bless ye, lad, bless ye!"

Noll's homeward walk seemed somewhat brighter to him, even though he left the child dead behind him. Dirk's gratitude, a small matter though it may have been, gave him a thrill of pleasure. It was pleasant to think that he had one friend among the fish-folk, rough and ignorant though they were. He remembered how, in the little sea-town in which his father had once dwelt, the fishermen came at last to love and respect the kind minister who worked so patiently to raise them out of their slough of ignorance and degradation, and that whenever his father walked among them, they flocked about him to listen to his words and counsel, and watch for his look or smile of approval.

"And," thought Noll, "if Uncle Richard would only do as papa did, what a happy man he would be, and what good he could do for Culm!" But that time — if ever it came — was yet a long, long way off, he thought, and so the people must live on their old, dreary, wretched life till some one taught them better.

The boy walked soberly home, with a great many serious, earnest thoughts in his heart. Somehow, this morning's sight had made another impression upon his mind beside that of sadness and disappointment. He felt and saw that there was a great work to do. Who was to do it?

Hagar met him at the door, rejoicing that he had returned in safety, but, stopping only to tell her that the child was dead, Noll went on to the library. It was the boy's intention to open his heart to his uncle, and tell him of all the want and wretchedness there was at Culm, while the impression was so deep and vivid in his mind; but Trafford sat at the organ and took no notice of his nephew's presence, and, after a long lingering, Noll gave up the attempt for that day, at least.

It was late in the afternoon when he went out for his accustomed walk. Partly by accident, partly by design, he came to the little place of graves in the frozen sand, and there found the funeral party from the fish-huts just gathering about the shallow resting-place which had been scooped for Dirk's treasure. The huddling crowd of poorly-clad men and women respectfully made way for him, and Dirk looked unutterable thanks for what he considered a great honor. Without a prayer, without a word of consolation, the little one was lowered into the earth amid the wailing of the women, and the shrill and lonely screaming of the fierce and bitter wind.

Noll had never seen anything so unutterably dreary, and when all was over, and the mourners had disappeared over the other side of the Rock, he went home, thinking more deeply than ever of the work to be done, and wondering who was to do it.

CHAPTER XII.

FIRELIGHT TALK.

THE warmth and quietness of the library made such a bright and pleasant contrast to the dreary scene in the Culm burying-ground that Noll gave a great sigh of pleasure and relief as he entered the room and found it light and cheerful with the blaze of a brisk fire on the hearth. He sat down in one of the big arm-chairs which stood either side of the fireplace, and held his numbed hands in the warmth, and looked about him, thinking that the old stone house was a palace in comparison with the other Culm habitations. Uncle Richard sat in his usual seat by the window, with his face toward the darkening sea, and, with the dismal scene which he had just witnessed fresh in his mind, Noll felt a tenderer yearning toward the stern man, — feeling, somehow, as if they could not be too near and dear to each other on this lonely Rock, where, just now, it seemed as if there was little else than wretchedness. Perhaps it was this feeling which led the boy to leave his seat and stand by his uncle's chair, and, with one hand on the grim man's shoulder, to say, "Dirk's child is dead, Uncle Richard, and they've just buried it. Oh! what a lonely place to be buried in! I would rather lie in the sea, it seems to me."

Trafford turned suddenly about at these words, exclaiming, "Hush, hush! don't talk about death, boy! What have you been up to that dreary little heap of graves for?"

"Partly to please Dirk, — partly because I wished, Uncle Richard. It's a dismal place! I'm glad enough to get back."

"We shall both sleep there soon enough," said Trafford, who seemed to be in one of his gloomiest moods. "Why go there till we go for the last time?"

Noll's arm went about his uncle's neck. "Don't say such things!" he said. "Perhaps we'll not live here always, Uncle Richard; and, if we do have to be buried up there in the sand, heaven is just as near, after all."

Trafford looked at the boy's face, ruddy and glowing from the long walk in the wind, and sighed, —

"Yes, for you, Noll. But for me, — no, no!"

"Why, Uncle Richard?"

"Because — it is all dark, — dark! I have nothing, see nothing to hope for beyond."

"Why won't you try to hope?" said Noll, softly.

"Hush! it's no use. Your Aunt Marguerite bade me follow after her long ago. I did not try. Your father said almost the same, Noll. Yet here I am, — I have not tried, I see no light, there is no hope for me."

The crackle of the fire and the hoarse voice of the sea had the silence all to themselves for a long time. At last Noll said, —

"When papa died, he did not fear at all, Uncle Richard. He said it was only the end of his journey, and that I was to follow on in the same way till I got to him at last. And papa said the truth, Uncle Richard."

"Yes! he never said aught else, Noll, — never!"

"And," continued the boy, his face growing grave, "papa said I was never to forget God, and never to forget to help any of his creatures if they were in trouble, and, oh! Uncle Richard, I hope I never shall!"

"Ah!" said Trafford, thoughtfully, "your father ever had others' welfare at heart. I remember, when we were lads, how, one day, in coming from the woods with nuts and grapes, we passed a poor creature by the roadside, who seemed fainting with fatigue or hunger. We both laughed at the queer figure at first, and passed by merrily, and went on our way; but Noll's face grew graver and graver, I remember, and by and by he would turn about, in spite of me, and go all the long way back to empty his pockets of their pennies and bits of silver into the wanderer's lap. Yes, he had a heart for every unfortunate, and it was not closed against them as he grew older."

Again the room was silent, while the fire flickered and painted flame-shadows on the wall, and lit up the dusky corners with its red glow. Noll sat on the arm of his uncle's chair, and watched the quivering shapes, and, in fancy, went back over the sea to Hastings. It was something such a night as this, he remembered, that papa had bidden him farewell,—lying so calm and patient in the great south chamber, where people were stepping softly about, and speaking in whispers and sighs. And papa's dear arms had been around him till the last, Noll thought, with his eyes brimming, and seeming yet to feel their gentle pressure; and, as long as it could whisper, the dear voice had breathed love and solemn counsel and fervent prayer into his ears. Back to the boy came the vivid recollection of all the hushed voice had said, — all the injunctions, the earnest entreaties to follow in the path which led only heavenward, and his heart was so full that he longed to cry out, "Papa, papa! if I might only see your face in this dreary place!"

Trafford presently said, speaking his thoughts aloud, "It was an evil day that separated us. God only knows what I might have been, had I always lived in the sunshine of his pure, warm heart. Why are you so silent, Noll?"

The boy could not trust himself to speak, and Trafford suddenly saw that there were tears shining in his eyes. Noll felt his uncle's hand laid upon his head, and the stern voice said, with all the tenderness of which it was capable, —

"It's a hard life for you, Noll. I can see, — I know it."

"No, no!" said the boy, quickly, "it's not that, Uncle Richard! I was only thinking of — of papa, — that was all."

"What about him?" queried Trafford; "I never knew that you mourned before."

"Why," said Noll, chokingly, "papa told me so much, — so much that he wished me to do and be, — and it all came to me just then, as if he were saying it over again."

"What did he wish you to do and be?" Trafford quietly asked.

"He said that — that I should find Christ's work to do wherever I might be, and that I must do his work and follow him wherever I should go; and — and I'm a long way from that, Uncle Richard; though," Noll added, turning his face away from the shining firelight, "I do try to do it, and not forget him nor his work."

Again Trafford's hand was laid upon the boy's head, this time to stroke his curly locks away from his eyes, where the wind had blown them.

"Did he tell you aught of me?" he asked, presently.

"No, — only that if you ever found me, or I you, that I was to be your boy. Papa said you would care for me."

"He believed in me still! He trusted me!" said Trafford. "Alas! he knew not what a father I should make his child."

Noll slipped off the chair arm, saying, "Don't say that again, Uncle Richard. Papa trusted you, — so do I. And, if you please, will you go out to supper? Hagar called a long time ago. Come, Uncle Richard, don't look so gloomy! Papa smiled even when — when he was saying good-by to me."

The instant these words escaped Noll's lips he half regretted them. He had never before allowed his uncle to know that he thought him sad and gloomy, and he was not quite sure that the careless word would strike agreeably upon his ears. But Trafford only said, —

"Yes, Noll, I know. We will go out to supper," and rose from the chair and followed after his nephew.

The boy did his best to make the meal a cheery one, thinking to himself that this, as much as anything, was a part of the work which papa wished him to do; and, observing his efforts, Trafford endeavored to keep pace with his nephew's cheerful talk. Noll did not go back to the library after tea was over, but followed Hagar out to her kitchen as she went thither with her tray of dishes, and sat down in the cozy corner by the fireplace. Somehow, the boy thought, the old housekeeper's humble kitchen seemed to gather more brightness and cheerfulness into its rough and smoke-tarnished precincts than the great library, with all its comforts and elegancies, ever held. The reason for this he did not seek; he only knew that it was so, and liked the wooden seat in the chimney-corner accordingly. Hagar came out with her last tray-load from the dining-room, and set it down upon the table with, —

"Bress ye, honey, Hagar's glad 'nough to see ye sittin' dar. 'Pears like I never heard de sea shoutin' like it is dis yer ebenin'. Seems as ef all de folks dat de cruel ole monster hab swallered wur jes' openin' the'r moufs and cryin' 'loud! Hagar t'anks de Lord dat yer ain't in de bottom ob it, honey."

The old housekeeper took two or three side glances at the boy's sober face as she poured the hot water over her dishes, and said at last, "Now don' ye s'pose Hagar knows what ye're t'inkin' ob so hard, chile? Ki! she c'u'd tell ye quicker'n nuffin. You's t'inkin' ob dem mis'able Culm folks, you is."

"You are partly right," said Noll. "It seems to me as if I couldn't think of anything else. I try to sometimes, but the sight of their wretched ways keeps coming to me, and it's no use to try and put it away. Oh, dear, I wish something could be done for them!"

"Dat's yer bressed father all ober!" said Hagar. "'Spects ef he was 'live an' livin' on dis yer wild'ness, we'd see somethin' did fur 'em. But Mas'r Dick — well, his heart is all frizzed up, jes' as I telled ye afore. But de Lord'll open it sometime, honey, — Hagar's got faith 'nough to b'lieve dat!"

"Oh! I hope so," said Noll; "but what are the people going to do till then?"

"Can't tell ye nuffin 'bout dat," said Hagar, making a vigorous clatter among her dishes; "'spects the day's comin', tho', when de Lord gets ready fur't. 'Tain't till *he* says, honey."

Noll gravely replenished the fire from the great basket of cones and chips which stood on the hearth, and stood listening, for a little time, to their brisk snap and crackle, then turned to Hagar, saying,—

"Do you think I could do anything for them, Hagar? I've been thinking this long time about it, and there's no one to ask but you, for I can't quite get courage enough to say anything to Uncle Richard about it,—he would be angry, I'm afraid. Do you think I could do anything, Hagar?"

The old housekeeper let go her dish-cloth, and turned about to look at Noll, as he stood before the fire. Her eyes surveyed the lad from head to foot,—as if it was the first time she had seen him,—and after a few minutes of silence she slowly said, "What put dat in yer head, chile?"

"I don't know; it's been there this great while. It was the misery over there, I suppose," said Noll.

"Well, well," said she, turning back to her dishes, "Hagar's 'stonished, she is! Does I 'spect ye ken do anything fur dem yer? Bress de Lord! *He'll* help ye, honey! — he'll help ye! An' ef it wa'n't de Lord dat put it in yer head — Well, chile," Hagar added, "de Lord's ebery-where, an' 'pears to me like as ef it was his doin'. What ye t'ink, honey?"

Noll was looking in the rosy bed of coals, and for a few minutes made no reply; then he said, in answer to Hagar's question, —

"I'd like to think that, Hagar. I'd like to have all my thoughts and plans come from him, and I'd like to do the Lord's work; for that's what I promised, — that's what I am trying to do."

Hagar wiped a pile of plates, and laying down her towel, said, reverently, —

"Promise, chile? Did ye promise de Lord, or who?"

After she had asked this question, she looked furtively over her shoulder at Noll, as if fearing she had asked about something which she had no right to know.

But Noll, with hands clasped over knee, was looking straight into the firelight, and did not appear offended; and pretty soon he said, slowly and softly, Hagar stopping her clatter to listen,—

"Before mamma died— Did you know mamma, Hagar?"

"Not muchly, chile," said Hagar; "yer Uncle Dick's wife was my lady."

"Well, before mamma died," continued Noll, "we used to take long walks upon the shore by the town. A great shining shore it was, I remember, and yellow like gold sometimes when the sun shone upon it."

"Like de shore ob de new Jerusalem," interposed Hagar, gazing abstractedly in her dish-pan.

"And there were great cedars and pines drooping down from the rocks," continued Noll, "and here mamma and I used to walk up and down when papa was busy in his study; and almost always he used to come out to walk a little with us before we were through. And one day we waited a long time for him to come out, and at last sat down on a rock, for mamma was not well then, and could not walk long without a rest; and as she looked across the smooth water, she said, 'And the building of the wall of it was of jasper: and the city was pure gold, like unto clear glass.' Though I was a good deal smaller than I am now, I knew what she meant, and of what she was thinking, for mamma used to talk about leaving me then; and I laid my head in her lap and cried a little, and said,—

"'Oh, don't talk of that, mamma, for what am I going to do?'"

Noll choked a little here at the remembrance, and Hagar drew a long breath.

"Then," continued Noll, with a quivering voice, "she bent her face over me and the tears in her eyes ran over on to my cheeks, and she said,—

"'Oh, my little Noll, if mamma could feel sure that you were ready to come after her into that city, she would never cry or mourn again!'

"It seemed as if my heart would break to see her cry and to know that I was *not* ready, and that I could not stop her tears. I wanted to scream and groan, my heart swelled so."

"Ob course ye did," said Hagar, with ready sympathy.

Noll was silent for a long minute. Somehow, the talk with Uncle Richard in the library had brought back the remembrance of all these past events so brightly and vividly that it was like living them over again. But he had not yet got to the "promise," and Hagar was waiting patiently. So he continued, with a slight effort, saying, —

"Mamma dried her tears very suddenly, for papa came in sight just then, and I suppose she feared he would be worried or anxious about her, and though she said nothing more to me about the city to which she was going, I couldn't forget her tears, nor that she was sorrowful and unhappy on my account. It made me miserable. I didn't want to walk with her the next day, for fear I should see her tears again; and I knew I could not bear *that*. So when it came time to go, I hid away, and she went alone."

"Poor honey!" said Hagar, reflectively.

"But that only made it all worse. I knew that I was all wrong, and that I ought to try and find Jesus, through whom, mamma said, she could only enter into the city. But it seemed as if he had hidden away from me; and the way was all dark and I was afraid and wretched and miserable."

"Oh, chile," said Hagar, "de bressed Lord was waitin' an' ready to take ye up in his arms de berry minnit ye frowed yerself on his mercy!"

"Yes," said Noll, "but I was not ready. I held back, and was wicked and wretched; but it couldn't last alway, and one night when I had said my prayer and been tucked in bed by mamma's poor weak, patient hands, I could delay no longer, and throwing my arms about her neck when she bent down to kiss me, I cried and sobbed, and begged her to help me find Jesus, who reigned over the city, and mamma cried too, — tears of joy they were, she said, — and told me that I had not to seek for him as for a great stranger, but that he stood ready to enter in and dwell in my heart the moment I yielded it up to him."

"Dat was de bressed troof!" said Hagar, with shining eyes; "an' what did ye do den, honey?"

"Mamma called papa to come, and he prayed that Jesus would forgive me and make my heart his own, and help me to always walk in the path that ends at last at the gate of his city. And," Noll added, turning partly about to Hagar, "I did give up, and — and I think he forgave me. The dreary load went off my heart, and I promised Jesus then to never forget him nor his work. When mamma did at last go to the city, I promised her the same; when papa went, I promised him too. That is my promise," said Noll, a little tremulously. "Do you think I can forget it, Hagar? Do you think I can help wanting to do what is his work?"

Hagar wiped her eyes. "'Spects dere's no need ob answerin' dat question," said she, quietly; "when de Lord's wid ye, dar ain't nobody gwine to 'vent yer workin' good, nohow."

"But I don't know how to begin," said Noll, "even if I could do anything. There's so much to be done, and I've nothing to do with. And I'm afraid that Uncle Richard will forbid me to do anything about it. He doesn't want me to go to Culm, he says, and he dislikes the Culm people."

Hagar did not know what consolation to offer for this unfavorable prospect. She could not counsel the boy to disobey his uncle's commands, neither did she accept the idea of having Noll's projects defeated for lack of permission to carry them out.

"Don' know, honey," said she, after a long meditation; "can't tell ye nuffin 'bout dat, nohow. But jes' go right on wid yer plans, an' de Lord'll find a way fur ye. He ken do it,—he ken do it, chile."

But the question was not settled in Noll's mind. It was not a thing to be undertaken without much deliberation, and, as yet, only the vaguest of schemes floated through his mind. He wished to aid, he longed to be doing something of the work that was to be done, but there did not seem to be the smallest prospect of a commencement.

Christmas came and went. The eve was not an unpleasant one to Noll, though he remembered all too well what a blithe evening the last Christmas-eve had been, and could not help thinking yearningly of the dear friends gathered merrily together across the sea, and wonder whether he was missed from the throng, as he sat by the fire all the solitary evening.

CHAPTER XIII.

THE WINTER'S WANING.

DIRK'S little one was not the only fever-stricken sleeper that was laid to rest in the dreary little burying-ground that winter. The fever, born of want and filth and exposure, lingered among the wretched huts, taking down the strong men and wasting the lives of the little ones, till, after weary lingering, they flickered out. Of course the sick ones had but the poorest of care and the rudest of medical aid. The people were disheartened and apathetic, and seemed to have no idea of cleansing their habitations or reforming their way of living. Noll once ventured to hint to Dirk, with whom he was more intimately acquainted than the others, that cleanliness and care might do much toward ridding them of the haunting fever. The fisherman stared blankly at this suggestion, and replied, —

"It mought do fur the like o' ye, lad; but we be poor folks, an' I don't think 'tw'u'd do the good ye think. The fever be come, an' it be goin' to stay till we be all lyin' up in the sand yender."

So the sickness lingered, meeting no resistance and no attempts to check its progress. It smote heaviest the little ones just toddling about, and who had not enough of strength and endurance in their little bodies to resist the slowly-destroying fever. So Dirk's treasure did not sleep alone in the sand, for many another father's was there to keep it company. Oh! the weariness of the days, the slow dragging of the weeks! When the sickness seemed to have spent itself, and hope was beginning to flicker up, back came the destroyer and fell upon some little one whom father and mother had fondly hoped to save, — for these Culm people, dull and ignorant though they were, had a strong and passionate love for their children that showed itself most vividly in these days of death, — and then the people settled into their old apathetic despair and found no light nor comfort for their souls.

Was it any wonder that — with all this misery and death about him, and the sight of it distressing him — Noll should grow sick at heart? The gloom of the old stone house and the desolateness of his new home, when compared with the one which he had left, had, at first, been all that his fresh young spirits could bear; and, having grown to like his new abode in a measure, he found, even then, that it would not do to remember Hastings and his friends too often; and now, in these dreary days, the boy began to grow less cheerful and to feel an unconquerable desire to go back to those who loved him and whose homes knew nothing of dreariness or gloom. This longing for friends he kept bravely to himself, because he thought it was a part of his work — the work which it seemed to him was God's — to be as brave and cheerful as possible before Uncle Richard, and win him out of his gloom and moroseness. So this yearning and desire for brighter scenes and faces was kept a secret, and Trafford suspected nothing of it. His keen eyes, however, detected that Noll was graver and less talkative than usual, and he began to look about for a reason. Some dim knowledge of the sickness and death in the village had crept in to him through Noll's and Hagar's talk, and a sudden fear chilled him lest his nephew, too, was to be stricken down with the lingering fever. What if it should be so? What if even now the boy was oppressed with the languor and depression which precedes illness? With this thought torturing him, he called to Noll one afternoon from the library window, as the boy was idly walking up and down the frozen sand. After a few minutes of waiting, Noll made his appearance at the library door, looking a little surprised, perhaps, at this unusual summons. Trafford bade him come up to his chair, and Noll obeyed.

"Where were you all the forenoon?" questioned the uncle. "I saw you but once after breakfast."

Noll looked as if he had much rather refrain from answering, but said, after a few seconds of hesitation, "Over at Culm, Uncle Richard."

"At Culm!" exclaimed Trafford, sternly. "Isn't the fever raging there?"

"Yes, sir."

"And you have been exposing yourself? Speak, Noll!"

"Why—yes—I suppose so, Uncle Richard. I was in the room where Hark Darby's little boy was sick."

Trafford stamped upon the floor with impatience. "What were you there for?" he cried.

"To carry something that Hagar made for it to drink. There's no doctor, you know; and they're terribly poor, Uncle Richard. Oh! if you could only —"

"Stop! I wish to hear naught of those fish-folks," cried Trafford. "Oh! you careless lad, what can I do with you? Are you determined to catch the fever? Are you bound to be always in danger?"

"No; but it's terrible over there, and — and they're dying with the sickness, and nothing to make them comfortable! Oh! how can I help it, Uncle Richard?"

Trafford looked into the lad's earnest eyes and sighed. "Would you like to take the fever and be buried with the rest up there in the sand?" he asked.

Noll shivered a little, and answered,

"No, I don't want to die, Uncle Richard. But I think I ought to help them all I can, over there, for all that. And it's such a little — such a *very* little — that I can do! Oh! Uncle Richard, don't you think it is terrible to see them so wretched, and no one to help them?"

"I don't see them!" said Trafford; "I should know nothing of it but for you, and I don't want you to see them or know aught of the misery or the sickness. Do you understand?"

Noll looked at his uncle as if he failed to comprehend.

"You don't mean that I'm not to go there any more?" he said.

"Yes, since you are not disposed to incline to my wishes, I must command you. You are not to go near—"

This time it was Noll who interrupted.

Before Trafford could finish his command, the boy had taken two or three quick steps forward and clasped his arms so quickly and convulsively about the stern man's neck that he was startled into silence.

"Don't, don't say that, Uncle Richard!" cried Noll; "I couldn't mind you if you did! It wouldn't be right, — when they're all sick and almost starving, — and I couldn't do it, and it is not as papa told me to do! And —"

Trafford endeavored to release Noll's hold, but the boy only clung the tighter, exclaiming, —

"No, no! don't say it, Uncle Richard, for I couldn't mind you! Papa never would wish me to! And oh, why don't *you* help those poor, dying people? Why don't you help them, Uncle Richard? Why don't you, — why *don't* you?"

Surprised at this unusual vehemence on the part of his nephew, Trafford was silent, hardly knowing whether to be angry or indifferent. That this matter lay very near the boy's heart, he had no longer any doubt. What could he do with him?

"Noll," said he after a long silence, "do you mean that you will not obey me?"

The boy hesitated. "In everything else, Uncle Richard," he answered, with red cheeks and downcast eyes; "but this—but this—oh, how can you ask me to stop? There isn't any one else to do anything, and it helps a little, and they look for me to come every day; and if I did not—oh, Uncle Richard, it would be too cruel! I can't do it! Do *you* think papa would be pleased?"

"But you are mine, now, not his," said

Trafford, with something like displeasure in his tone; "aren't you aware of it?"

Noll said not a word, but stood with his eyes turned away from his uncle's, and his cheeks crimsoning, while his breath came quick and fast.

"Will you obey me or not?" Trafford asked, sternly.

Noll turned around and met his uncle's eye. He began to plead. His awe of his uncle seemed to have vanished for the time, and Trafford was astonished at the boy's earnestness and vehemence. Two or three times he was about to put up his hand to command silence, but Noll redoubled his pleading, and he continued to listen. All the remembrances of the past dreary weeks—the want, the slow wasting, the flickering out of life, the dismal laying away of the poor body in the sand

—came to Noll as vividly as the reality which he had witnessed, and made him pray for relief with an earnestness and entreaty which ordinarily were not his.

"Just think, Uncle Richard," said he, in conclusion, "papa would have gone to their aid long ago. He bade me do all the good I could, and you won't forbid me?—oh, I know you will not!—and won't you help me to do more,—won't you, Uncle Richard?"

Trafford gloomily pushed his nephew away.

"Go!" he said; "I do not care to see you any more this afternoon."

Hardly had the boy turned away, however, before the quick thought flashed into his mind that he had failed to ask him the question for which he had called him. He might even now be ill, and he was sending him away in anger!

"Noll!" exclaimed Trafford, "come back. Are you ill, my boy?"

"No, sir."

"Why are you so grave and sober of late?"

"I didn't know that I was, Uncle Richard."

Trafford looked keenly in his nephew's face, and at last drew him toward himself. What if the fever should get a hold of the boy? he thought, anxiously. There was no aid, no succor!

"Oh, Noll," he said, as tenderly as he might, "you cannot know what a blow it would be to me to lose you. Won't you be careful for my sake?"

"Yes, Uncle Richard; I don't think there is much danger, though. It is only the weak, half-starved ones that are ill."

A long silence followed. Then Noll asked, softly,—

"Do you give me permission to help them all I can, Uncle Richard?"

Trafford drew a great sigh, as if he felt himself to be yielding, perhaps, the boy's very life, and answered, "Yes."

"And you'll help me, too?" said Noll, brightly.

"No! Isn't this enough? What more would you have?"

"I thought that — that perhaps you would help a little, too,—you can do so much more than I," said Noll.

Trafford shook his head, gloomily. "No," he said; "I can give you nothing but money. I have no heart for the work. And now I think of it, you've had no allowance since you came here, Noll. I had not thought of it before. Brother Noll and I always had spending-money."

"But I've no use for it," said Noll,

with a little laugh; "I couldn't spend it if I tried, Uncle Richard!"

"You may find a use for it when the 'Gull' begins her trips again," said his uncle; "at any rate, you shall have an allowance. You will find it on your study table every Monday morning."

Noll thanked his uncle for this kindness, but at the time, was much at a loss what to do with his weekly allowance which every Monday morning brought him. He found a use for it, however, as time will show.

After this long talk, Noll felt somewhat lighter-hearted, if for no other reason than because he had received Uncle Richard's permission to go on with his work of aid. Spring was not far off, and with its coming the fever would most likely flee, and then, he thought, there would be some hope of doing something for the Culm people. And was he not already doing something?

To Noll, it seemed but the merest trifle; in the eyes of the poor fish-folk, his deeds were great and wonderful. All unconsciously, the boy was accomplishing one of the most difficult portions of the task which he had set for himself,—the winning of those rough, untaught hearts. Many an uncouth blessing was called down upon the lad's head as he made his appearance day after day at the doors of the habitations which the fever had entered. His cheery, gladsome presence, the Culm folk thought, was like a ray of sunshine in the gloom of their hovels. It was curious to see how those great brawny men confided in him, and watched to see him coming down the sands of a morning-time, with his basket of delicacies on one arm, balanced by a basket of more substantial food on the other. Not one of the men but what, in their hearts, loved the boy and blessed the day which brought him to Culm Rock. And, quite before he was aware of it, Noll had accomplished one great object, and won the love and confidence of the fish-folk.

The snow melted and ran into the sea, the ice in the rock hollows trickled its life away, and warmer winds and sunnier clouds gave token of the spring's coming; and Noll grew happier every day and looked gleefully forward to the coming of the "Gull," and the tidings which she would bring. Often in these days, when returning from his morning round, it seemed to the boy as if his own father's blessing rested upon his heart, it was so light and glad, and that God's love was all about him and smiling over the barren Rock and the far, wide sea.

CHAPTER XIV.

NED THORN.

IT was on one of the balmiest of spring afternoons that Noll went over to Culm to see a little child who was recovering from the fever. The sickness, apparently, had run its course, and the people were beginning to take heart; and the men were overhauling their nets and making ready for their summer's work. There had been a heavy storm on the previous evening, and Noll found quantities of brilliant sea-weeds and curious shells and pebbles on his walk along the beach, and lingered long to search for treasures and enjoy the bright loveliness of the day. Culm Rock and the great sea had never looked fairer to him than on this afternoon, — the one lying warm and silent, its great stone ribs purpling under the sun, and the other flecked with curling ripples of snowy foam and emerald light.

It was late afternoon when he arrived at the Culm houses, and so long did he linger that the sun was dipping in the waves before he was ready to leave his little patient. He was standing in the door, swinging his basket to and fro, and on the point of taking his departure, when a sudden shout of voices from without turned his attention in that direction. There, slowly riding in over the waves all burnished and aflame with ruddy sunlight, was the "Gull"!

For a few short seconds Noll actually stood still with pleasure and delight, then dropping his basket, he ran off across the sand toward the wharf, as fast as he could go. The fishermen were already congregating there, and their wives were standing in the doors of their dwellings to gaze upon the welcome sight.

The vessel's white wings slowly brought her round to the little wharf, revealing the skipper's sturdy person, and Mr. Snape's long and solemn visage. Noll could hardly wait for the craft to touch the planks, and Skipper Ben spied the lad before the "Gull" came up, with a dull thump and jar, alongside.

"Great fishes!" cried he, extending his hand to aid Noll in clambering aboard, "if here ben't the lad, alive an' hearty! Glad ter see ye,—glad ter see ye!" shaking the boy's hand as if he never would have done.

"You may believe I'm glad to see you!" said Noll; "I never was so glad to see anything as the old 'Gull' in my life; and oh, why didn't you come earlier, skipper?"

Ben laughed. "I knowed ye hev a hard time on't," he said; "reckoned ye'd be glad ter see the old skipper once more. An', lad, how goes it?"

Mr. Snape came up just here, drawling, "What ye think o' the winters down 'ere, now, lad?"

"They *are* long," said Noll; "but I've got through one, somehow. If it weren't for the sickness, and such a long time without letters, I wouldn't mind. Oh! skipper, haven't you got a great packet of 'em for me?"

"Been sick down 'ere; hev ye?" said Ben, evading Noll's question. "Well, that's wuss'n bein' without letters, eh, lad?"

"But haven't you got a bundle of 'em for me?" queried Noll. "I can't wait, skipper!"

The skipper began to slowly shake his head. "Sorry," he said, "but I didn't bring ye nary letter this time. Don' know but all yer frien's hev forgot ye, fur they didn't give a single scrap o' paper to bring, nor a message, nuther."

Mr. Snape began to grin, seeing how Noll's face fell, and how all his joy and eagerness had suddenly vanished, and stepping along to the hatchway, made certain mysterious signs and beckonings to something or some one there. Noll, filled with disappointment, walked away to the stern and looked down into the green depths of water rippling there, and strove to conceal his feelings from the watchful skipper. Up from the hatchway and along the deck came a light step, — eager, hurrying, — and before Noll could turn around, two arms had clasped him about and held him fast against the rail, while a voice — just as full of laughter and merriness as a voice could be — cried, —

"Oh, Noll, Noll Trafford! not to know me! not to *guess* that I was here! Why, you dear old fellow, ain't I better than letters? I've a good mind to never let you look around to pay for not mistrusting that I was here! Oh, Noll!"

"Well, I be beat!" said the skipper. "I never seed a lad so dumbfounded afore. What ye goin' to give me fur bringin' ye sech a parcel, Master Noll?"

But Noll had only eyes and ears for his friend.

"Ned, Ned Thorn!" he exclaimed, looking at his friend with wide-open eyes, as if he thought he was seeing a vision. "It is really you, only grown a little taller!"

"Of course it is; who else should it be?" said Ned, drawing his friend out to one of the skipper's bales, where they could both sit down. "You're brown as an old salt, Noll; but you haven't grown a bit! Oh, but you may believe I'm glad to see you! I thought you'd be dying by this time to see some one from Hastings, and when the skipper pointed out the old stone dungeon where you live, I thought likely you were dead already. What a horrid old fortress 'tis! and weren't you awful homesick? and aren't you terribly moped up in such quarters? and, you dear old Noll, how *have* you managed to live it through, anyhow?"

"Beats everything at questions, that lad does," observed Mr. Snape to the skipper; "nigh about pestered me to death, comin' down. You'd better charge double ef yer goin' to carry him home, 'cause it's two days' work fur one man ter tend to his talk. I ben't goin' to do't fur nothin'."

"They ben't glad to see each other, eh, Jack?" said Ben; "wish there was some prospect o' taking t'other home, too."

"I sh'u'd be 'feared the 'Gull''d founder," said Mr. Snape.

Noll, in the midst of happy talk, suddenly recollected that it was after sundown, and that Uncle Richard and the tea-table would be waiting.

"Come, Ned," he said, gleefully, "I'd forgotten all about sunset and home till this minute. It's a good long walk, and we must start."

"I'm ready," said Ned, jumping up. "Skipper, where's my carpet-bag? I'm going to stay, Noll, just as long as you'll keep me; and now I'm anxious for a look inside your old dungeon and a peep at that grim old — that's what the skipper said he was — uncle of yours. Do you think he'll scold because I've come?"

"Indeed not!" said Noll; "and Uncle Richard's not so very grim, either. We'll have splendid times in the old house, and now see if you aren't sorry when it comes time for you to leave Culm Rock."

They clambered over the "Gull's" side on to the wharf, and passed through in the little lane which the fishermen made for them, to the smooth and shining sand, and so started for the stone house.

Ned Thorn was a boy of Noll's own age, and much resembled him in appearance, though, of the two, Ned was a trifle the taller. Indeed, as Mr. Snape observed, leaning over the rail and smoking his pipe while he watched the two lads walking briskly homeward, —

"They're as like as two peas, Ben,—did ye note?—only one's more so than t'other."

It seemed to Noll, while on this homeward walk, that nothing was lacking to make home pleasant, now that Ned had come. His friend's presence did not seem a reality, as yet, and he had to listen a long time to Ned's merry chatter before he could realize that it was actually Ned Thorn who was walking beside him in this purple twilight, along the shore of the glimmering, sounding sea.

"What a queer place!" said Ned, stopping, at the curve of the shore, to look off at the horizon, which seemed to rise higher than their heads, and turning to look at the dark wall of rock behind them; "and what a lonesome sound the waves make! I should have died of the blues in three weeks. And what a miserable set those fishermen are! They all seem to like you, though. Did you see how they made way for us, and touched their caps, some of them? What a capital place to fish, off those rocks! I'm glad I brought hooks and lines, and — What's that light ahead? A lighthouse?"

"No, only Hagar's kitchen window,"

said Noll; "Hagar's our black cook, and there's only three of us in that great house, Ned!"

"I should think you'd lose each other! Is your uncle like your father at all?"

"No, Uncle Richard's not much like papa," said Noll, with sudden graveness; "but he loves me, and—and I hope you'll like him, Ned."

They walked the rest of the way in silence till they came to the piazza steps under the shadow of the great stone house.

"It looks just as it did when I saw it first," said Noll,—"the sea getting dark and shadowy and making that lonesome sound on the pebbles, and oh, how I had to rap and search before I could find my way in! But come on, Ned."

Noll led his friend along the echoing

hall, straight to Uncle Richard's library, where the lamp had been lighted.

"This is Ned Thorn, Uncle Richard," said he, as they entered, "and he's come clear from Hastings to see me."

"Ned is very welcome," said Trafford, who chanced to be in a cheerful mood, "and if you boys are ready, we will go out to tea."

Noll ran on before to Hagar's kitchen, where he burst in, exclaiming,—

"Another plate and teacup, Hagar! Did you know that we have actually got company? It's Ned Thorn, a dear friend of mine, and he's from Hastings, and going to stay—I don't know how long. Will you bring them? Is tea all ready?"

"Bress ye!" said Hagar, "I's 'stonished to see ye so 'cited, honey. I'll bring de dishes in a minnit."

The old housekeeper followed him back to the dining-room, where the new-comer was endeavoring to interest Trafford in the account of the day's journey, telling it in such a sprightly manner that the grim master was betrayed into more than one smile.

"And now, Mr. Trafford, I'm going to stay here in this dismal old house just as long as you'll keep me," said Ned, in conclusion. "And Noll and I are going to have tip-top good times! I don't know as there's a thing we can have fun out of, but if there isn't, we'll invent something. We can fish,—there's one consolation! Why, Mr. Trafford, what does Noll do with himself, anyhow? I think he's grown as sober as — as — I don't know what!"

"Very likely," said Trafford, with a shadow of gloom on his face; "this is a sober place. Noll has seen much of which you know nothing, and it has made him graver and more thoughtful, I suppose; yet—"

"Yet you think he's all the better for that?" said Ned, merrily. "Well, so do I! Papa always says I'm too much of a rattle-box; but I can't help it. I couldn't be sober, like Noll, if I should try; and you wouldn't want me to; would you, old fellow?"

Noll looked as if he was entirely suited, now, and secretly wondered what Uncle Richard thought of his merry, light-hearted friend. The days which followed were happy ones. Trafford recollected that Noll had had a long winter of study, and granted a vacation to last during Ned Thorn's stay; so the two boys were at liberty to fish and ramble and explore rock and sand to their hearts' content. They gathered basket after basket full of sea flowers and weeds of vivid dye, to be pressed and packed for transportation to Hastings, and such quantities of shells, with an occasional pebble of agate or carnelian, that Ned laughingly declared,—

"I'll have just all the baggage the 'Gull' can float under, Noll. I'll have to charter it to convey me and mine; for the skipper won't take me under any other condition, you may be sure."

And these days were merry ones too. Hagar declared, "Dat yer Thorn boy beat eberyt'ing dis ole woman eber seed. 'Peared like ther' was more'n forty boys racin' up an' down dem yer stairs, an' laughin' at de tops ob ther voices. Neber seed nuffin like it, nohow! But is ye sorry, Hagar? Ye knows ye isn't! Ye likes to hear dis yer ole house waked up an' 'pear as ef 'twas good fur somethin' 'sides holdin' mis'ry."

Noll more than once trembled lest Uncle Richard should be displeased at this unusual clamor and mirthfulness, and banish Ned in anger; but day after day passed, and Trafford made no opposition to the boys' plans or proceedings, and apparently took quite a fancy to Noll's friend.

"I'd just like to coax your uncle into playing a game of ball with us," said Ned, as the two sat on the piazza one evening at twilight; "do you suppose he would consent?"

"Uncle Richard play ball!" exclaimed Noll, laughing at the idea. "No! I would almost as soon expect to see this old stone house playing at toss and catch."

"Well, he *is* the strangest man!" observed Ned; "but he loves you, — I can see that, every day, — and perhaps he'll come out as bright as a dollar, by and by. And — do you remember? — you was to tell me about that plan to-night. Go in, Noll dear, — I'm all attention."

CHAPTER XV.

PLANS.

NOLL looked thoughtfully on the sea a few minutes before he said, "I don't know what you'll say, Ned, the plan is so difficult; but I've thought of it a long time,—I believe it's been in my head every day for the last two months,—and it seems to me it is possible. Oh! if it *were*, I'd be the happiest boy in the land!"

"Well, now what have you got in your head, I'd like to know?" said Ned; "tell me quickly, for I hate long speeches, you know."

"Well, in the first place, you must know I want to help those Culm people, somehow. That's —"

"Yes," interrupted Ned, "they need 'helping,' I should think! They're the laziest, miserablest set of people I ever saw. Some of 'em need 'helping' with a good, sound punching, — 'twould stir 'em up a little."

"That's the object of the plan, and the next thing is how to do it," continued Noll. "If papa had only lived here a little time, I know it would have been a different place, and I want to make it what he would have made it; but, though I can't do that, I want to do something."

"I'll warrant you do!" said Ned, edging nearer his friend. "What do you think Hagar has told me about your work this winter? You *are* the funniest fellow, and I don't see what puts such ideas in your head, anyhow!—they never get into mine.'

"Well, I'll never get to my plan at this rate," said Noll, laughing a bit. "I don't believe the people will ever be any cleaner or more industrious till they have better houses to live in, and they're too poor to buy lumber and make repairs. Now, if I could only accomplish that, I think they'd soon have some pride in keeping their dwellings nice and neat, and that would keep the fever away, and perhaps—I almost *know*—they'd soon be a different people!"

"My stars!" exclaimed Ned, "what're

you thinking of? Do you really mean that — that you're going to repair their huts for them?"

"Yes, that is what I wish to do, and what I've been planning for," said Noll, peering through the dusk to see how Ned received the project; "and do you think I'll succeed?—do you think it is possible?"

Ned was silent a few seconds, and the low voice of the sea rose and murmured far up and down the beach-line and died away in a faint whisper before he replied, "Well, I *am* astonished! and if any one else had proposed it, I should say they were out of their wits. Now, what are those dirty fishermen to you, Noll?"

"That was not the question," said Noll. "Do you think I can succeed?"

"I don't know, — can't tell, — it's all so sudden. Where will you get the money?

and why don't your Uncle Richard do the work, instead of you?"

"Uncle Richard? why, he — he doesn't care for the Culm people," Noll was obliged to confess; "but as for the money, I think I can manage that. You see, he gives me more spending-money every week than I used to have in a whole quarter, — I showed you all my savings the other night, you remember, — and it has got to be quite a sum. Then I have about as much more that Mr. Gray gave me when I came away, and with this I'll make a commencement. The —"

"But what will your uncle say? Does he know?" queried Ned.

"No, he knows nothing about it. But he gave me permission, a long time ago, to aid the Culm people, and he lets me do as I choose with my money. So doesn't my plan seem possible?"

"Yes, if you can tell where lumber and nails and a carpenter are to come from," said Ned.

"Oh! but those will have to come down from Hastings, on the 'Gull,' of course. There's nothing here to do with," said Noll; "and I mean to coax Ben Tate to buy the lumber and hire a carpenter for me. You see, I've got it all planned, and if it will only work!"

"My stars!" said Ned, "I didn't know you were such a fellow. Why, I don't wonder these fish-folks all touch their hats to you, — they can afford to, I think. And, Noll, won't you tell me what these people are to you? I can't see, for the life of me! And why should you spend all your money for them?"

Noll hesitated, not feeling certain that Ned would understand his reason, if he told him, and, looking up at the stars, which had come out in great fleets over the sea, was silent. But Ned got up, came to Noll's end of the step, and, sitting down beside him, said, —

"Now for your reason! I'm not be put off at all. Won't you tell me?"

"Yes, if you wish very much to know," said Noll, in a lower tone. "I think everybody has a work to do, — a work that God gives them, — and I think this is mine, that he has given me. And I promised always to do his work, and I mean to do it, if I can. Besides," he added, softly taking Ned's hand in his, "it is work that papa would do if he were here, and I know that he, too, would be glad to have me do it. Wouldn't you be anxious to get about it at once, and without waiting for the Culm people to sink lower, if you thought it was your work and waiting for your hands? Wouldn't you, Ned?"

Noll's friend was suddenly silent. It was hardly such a reason as he had expected to hear, and what to reply he did not know. "Noll always was the funniest fellow ever since I knew him!" he thought to himself.

Noll waited, and tried to look into his friend's face, and feared that Ned did not comprehend his motives, after all. At last he said, "Don't you understand?"

"Oh, yes," said Ned, quickly, "but I —well—I didn't know what to say, and, somehow, you make me ashamed. It seems too bad for you to waste—spend, I mean —your money for those fishermen."

"Oh, no," said Noll, "I've no need of it for myself, and if I had, they need it more than I. And, Ned, I want to beg you to help me. Will you?"

"Pshaw! I'd be no help at all!" said Ned; "I'm no good at such things."

"But will you try?" said Noll, eagerly.

"Yes, if you wish. But I'll be sure to bother or make a mess of something, —see if I don't!"

At that instant the hall door behind them opened, and Trafford stepped out. So dark had it grown that he failed, at first, to see the two figures on the step; but when a little stir of Ned's betrayed them, he exclaimed, in a tone of great relief,—

"Ah, here you are, boys! I feared that —that you were up the shore, perhaps. Come in, come in. Why do you sit here in the darkness?"

"So I say!" said Ned, briskly, and

not regretting this interruption; "what *are* we sitting here in the dark for, Noll? Let's go in!"

As they were groping along their darksome way to the library, Ned whispered,—

"When are you going to begin your plan, or 'put it in execution,' as the books say?"

"The skipper will touch here to-morrow; I'd like to see him then," said Noll.

"Why not?" returned Ned. "We can get up early and run over to Culm before breakfast, and coax Ben into doing the business for you."

"We will!" said Noll, gladly, "and have the work begun at once; and I knew you'd be willing to help. Oh, Ned, I wish you were to stay here always."

The boys did not linger long in the library after arriving there, but went up to Noll's chamber, where his little hoard of money was brought forth and counted. Neither of the lads knew how far it would go toward purchasing lumber, but to them the sum in hand seemed a large one, and they decided, after much deliberation, to place it in Ben's hands, and trust to his judgment and discretion.

"But how is the carpenter to be paid for his labor, if this all goes for lumber?" queried Ned.

"Why, my spending-money is accumulating all the time," said Noll, "and though that won't be enough, I'll manage to get the rest, somehow. I'll write to Mr. Gray, or do something that will bring it."

They were both up at the first glimmer of dawn the next morning, and on their way to Culm long before the mist had fled from off the face of the sea. They ran, and made all possible haste, and were only just in time after all; for Ben was about to stand out on the day's journey as they came panting and breathless on to the little wharf.

"What be wantin' now, lads?" he cried, gruffly; "we be in a hurry to get off!"

"But you must wait a few minutes," said Ned, "for we want to come aboard, skipper. We can't run a mile for nothing, and before breakfast too."

"S'pose I shall hev ter!" grumbled Ben, as he gave them each a hand to help them up.

Noll brought forth his roll of money, and narrated his errand, disclosing for what object the lumber was to be purchased. Ben sat down and stared blankly at the boy, while Mr. Snape, who had drawn near, looked utterly bewildered.

"Let me hear ye say that agen," said Ben, when his scattered senses began to return; "I think I did not hear ye rightly."

Noll repeated his errand, aided by some impatient explanations which Ned threw in for the skipper's benefit.

"Well," said the "Gull's" master, as he concluded, "I be beat! Why, lad, 'tw'u'd be like throwin' yer silver into the sea to spend it on them good-fur-nothin', shif'less critters. An' what be the like o' them to you?"

"Why," said Ned, coming to Noll's relief, "he want's to do them good. Can't you see through a ladder, Ben? And what we want to know is whether you will do the business?"

The skipper was silent for a time. What was passing in his mind, the boys did not suspect, and they feared lest he should refuse. But presently he got up, saying, with gruffness which was assumed to hide a sudden tenderness in the old sailor's heart,—

"I ken do't fur ye, lad, I s'pose!—tho' I call ye foolish all the same. The 'Gull' be engaged fur the next run, but the next arter that ye shall hev yer boards an' yer carpenter."

"That will be week after next," said Ned. "Hurrah for you, Ben! And I want to engage a passage home for next week. Come, Noll, let's go back and let the skipper put out, if he's in such a hurry. A good voyage to you, Ben!—and don't you forget that I'm to go next week, now!"

"Ay, ay," said Ben, "get along with you!" and over the side went the boys, and, after a little delay, off went the "Gull" with Noll's precious savings on board.

"Wait," said Noll, as they left the wharf, "there's Dirk Sharp out there with his boat, ready to put off. Wait here, Ned, till I've spoken with him." And Noll ran off across the sand.

Ned sat down on the wharf and watched his friend and the fisherman. They were sufficiently near for him to note the expressions upon their faces, and when he saw the blank look of wonder and incredulity that suddenly came over Dirk's coarse features, he suspected that Noll was disclosing his project.

"Oh, but Noll *is* a queer fellow," he said to himself. "How can he care for these dirty, dull-witted fellows that can't spell their own names, when he is so smart and such a long, long way above them?"

But Noll, he remembered, had answered this question on the previous evening; yet Ned could hardly comprehend such motives, and so sat puzzling his head over it till his friend came back with a pleased and happy face, to say, —

"I'm ready now. You should have seen Dirk when I told what was going to be done! The great fellow almost cried before I could finish; and he's promised to aid me in a dozen ways, at least, and promised, oh! so much besides. And it seems as if I'll be the happiest boy in the world when once things are under way."

"I suppose you will be," said Ned, with something like a sigh, "and I wish I could stay and see how the huts'll look after you've done with them. However," he added, brightly, "I can come again sometime, — there's one consolation."

The fair spring days went on with the speed with which all happy days fly by, and little by little the Culm people began to talk among themselves of the — to them — great event which was to take place so soon. Noll overheard one old fish-wife say, "We ben't slick 'nough for new housen; ther'll hev to be great scrubbin' an' scourin' that day, eh, Janet?" to her slatternly daughter-in-law; and the boy mentally prayed that this opinion would gain ground among all the fish-folk. If there was only some one to teach the children, and save them from the utter ignorance which was their parents', there would be great hope for Culm, he thought.

Ned Thorn went home, and this was the only sad day which Noll knew during the two weeks' waiting. He could not bid Ned good-by and see the dear, merry face fade away, as the "Gull" departed, without a great choking in his throat and a heaviness of heart that made one day a lonely, homesick one.

CHAPTER XVI.

THE WORK BEGUN.

YOU may be sure that Noll did not fail to be at Culm village when the "Gull" and its precious freight arrived. The sky had been overcast all day and the sea somewhat rough, so that he was not certain that Ben would set sail from Hastings. But about half-past four in the afternoon the white wings of the skipper's craft hovered on the horizon, and soon after began to loom into shape and proportion. Noll first descried the welcome sight while standing on the piazza steps, anxiously surveying the sea and sky. A strong and vigorous breeze bore the "Gull" rapidly before it, and it was soon evident that it would arrive at the wharf before himself, unless he started soon. Recitations were over an hour ago, and he was now at liberty to go where he chose, and accordingly started for Culm at once. He arrived there some time before Ben and his craft, after all, and was forced to sit and wait impatiently. He could see the yellow lumber long enough before the "Gull" was in hailing distance, and knew that Ben had been successful.

The skipper came alongside at last, shouting at the top of his voice, "Ahoy, there, men! Give us a hand at this 'ere lumber, an' be spry about it, fur there's a storm brewin', an' I've got ter be twenty mile down the coast afore it breaks!"

The fishermen drew near at this summons, and as soon as the "Gull" was fast, they began to unload the cargo, under the carpenter's directions. It was carried well up the sand to preserve it from the dash of the sea and the treachery of the tide, and Noll stood looking on with a heart so full of joy and satisfaction that he forgot all about the skipper till a gruff voice cried, "Why don't ye come aboard, lad? Here be sumat fur ye that come from the city. It be a mighty thick letter, somehow. Give us yer hand an' come up, lad!"

Noll got aboard quickly enough after this intelligence, and took the packet which the skipper fished out from under his pea-jacket, saying, "I wonder if it can be from Ned?"

"How ken I tell?" said Ben, evasively. "Best open it, lad, — best open it."

Noll quickly had the envelope open, and, holding the packet upside down, there fell out upon the deck a thick little wad of bank-notes, which the wind threatened to take off into the sea before the boy's astonished senses returned to him. Ben prevented such a disaster, however, by picking up the roll and placing it in Noll's hand, with, "It's worth savin', lad, fur 'tain't every bush that grows sech blossoms, eh?"

"I should think not," said Noll, still full of amazement, and hurriedly opened his letter to see where this bounty hailed from, while Ben walked off to assist in his craft's unlading. This is what Noll's wondering eyes found: —

"HASTINGS, May 20th.

"DEAR NOLL,—I can imagine just how your eyes are staring by this time; but you needn't be alarmed, for I came by the money honestly. This is how it was: Papa said I might have a new pony if I would save my spending-money till I got a third of the sum which one would cost, and so, though I didn't hint of it to you when I was down at Culm, I've been laying up and laying up, like an old miser; and last Monday morning I found that I had got the sum, and so papa made up the rest to me. But when I thought of you and those miserable Culm people, and how you were making a fool of yourself (as Ben T. said), I thought I'd like to—to—well, let pony go, and help you a bit. So here's the whole sum (if you get it safe), and you're just as welcome as you can be, and don't you make any fuss about it, for it's your own, and I can go without spending-money if you can, and am willing to too. And it's no great denial, either, for the pony'll come sometime, I'm quite sure. So don't you worry any more about how the carpenter is to be paid. Good-by, dear old fellow,

"NED THORN.

"P. S.—I was just as dismal as I could be after I got home, longing to go back to that dreary, dismal, good-for-nothing Culm Rock. The shells, etc., got here all right. Give my respects to Uncle Richard, and tell him I'll come down and turn his house topsy-turvy for him again next summer, if he wants me to. Don't you forget to send a letter back by Ben, now."

Noll finished this characteristic letter with something very like tears in his eyes. "The dear, generous fellow!" he thought to himself; "how could he ever bring himself to do it? for it *is* a denial, because Ned is *so* fond of a horse! And he claimed, all the time, that he never could help at all!"

Ben came stumping along the deck with his gruff, "Well, we hev brought yer lumber an' yer carpenter, lad,—both on 'em the best I c'u'd find. One's 'bout stacked up on the sand, yender, and t'other'll be waitin' fur yer orders purty soon. He's good at his trade, John Sampson be, an' he'll do fair an' square by ye. John ben't delicate neither, an' won't mind the livin' he'll get 'mongst these 'ere good-fur-nothin's,—I looked out fur that, ye see."

"I thank you more than I can tell, Ben," said Noll, taking the skipper's hand; "and have you taken your pay for the freight and all the trouble?"

"The freight be paid fur," said Ben, "an' the trouble likewise. An' ef ye hev anythin' more fur the 'Gull' ter do, don't ye be backward, boy, about lettin' her know't."

The last of the lumber was now being dragged up the sand, and the skipper hurried away, saying,—

"Luck ter ye an' yer undertakin', lad! We be in a desput hurry to get off, fur we'd stan' a poor chance on this shore in a storm."

Noll wished the skipper a safe run to a better harbor, and went back to the wharf, where the carpenter intercepted him. He was a rough, blunt-spoken man, but was evidently "good at his trade," as Ben had said, and did not despair of making the Culm huts decent and habitable; and after a long talk with him, Noll started for home, as the afternoon was fast giving way to a gray and lowery night. His heart was full of gratitude and love to Ned, and he stopped more than once on his homeward walk to read the letter over by the gray glimmer of twilight. At first he was more than half resolved to return the money, and bid his friend to buy the pony,—it seemed such a great denial for horse-loving, mirthful Ned to make,—but as he read the letter again and again, and pondered over its contents, he began to think that his friend had more earnestness and love for kind-doing than he had ever suspected.

"I wronged the poor fellow," he thought

to himself, "because he was so merry and careless all the time. And now he's sent me this great roll of bills to help those people whom he pretended to hate! Oh, I wonder if it is best to keep them?"

This question was not decided then. It took more than one day's thought about the matter before he at last concluded to accept Ned's bounty, and perhaps he would not have decided thus at all if he had been quite sure that his friend would not be greatly grieved and offended at having the money returned.

Meanwhile, the carpenter commenced operations. Dirk's house was the first to undergo repairs, and Noll took every opportunity to go over to Culm to see how matters were progressing. It was a great delight to him to watch John Sampson at his labor, and note how saw and hammer and plane, guided by his strong and skilful hand, repaired the rents, brought the shackling doors and windows to comfortable tightness, made the crooked and twisted roofs to assume something like straight and even proportions, and righted matters generally. When Dirk's habitation was thoroughly repaired, it was the wonder and admiration of all the Culm people.

"It be like what it was when I was a gal, an' all the housen was new," said one old fish-wife, who had tottered in with the others.

"Ay, mother," said Dirk, "an' it be time we had new habits to go with the new housen, eh?"

Noll had not allowed any good opportunities, wherein he might hint to Dirk that cleanliness and industry should reign in the snug new quarters, to pass without improving them. Dirk, out of regard and gratitude to "the young master," as he called him, was willing to make the attempt, and strove, in his bungling way, to impress his neighbors with the fact that they were expected to reform their way of living. But it was up-hill work for people who had lived all their life in filth and wretchedness, and progressed but slowly. Many were the hours, after the recitations were over, that Noll spent over at the little village those warm days, planning with John Sampson about broken doors and shattered beams, which were to be made strong and serviceable, or, sitting on a pile of lumber, watching the carpenter as he put in execution the plans which they had made. The children of the village were generally playing near by, in the sand, with blocks and chips, — growing up as unlettered and ignorant as their parents. Some of them were great boys and girls, — almost as tall as Noll himself, — and had never yet seen the inside of a book.

"If Uncle Richard would only hire a teacher," thought Noll, "and have them grow up with some knowledge in their heads, they'd never get so low and wretched as their parents. But that nev-er'll be, I'm afraid. Oh! if I were only rich, how quick I'd change it all!"

But there was no prospect of any such fortune befalling him, and he usually turned away from the cluster of dirty, unkempt children with a hopeless sigh. He said, one day, while sitting on a great heap of shingles beside the carpenter, —

"What's to become of all these children, Mr. Sampson? Will they be left to grow up like their fathers and mothers?"

"Well, I don't see much to hinder," said the carpenter, with a glance at the dirty little ones who were throwing sand over their heads. "Don't think you'll ever see many lawyers and ministers out o' the lot."

"If there could only be a school here," continued Noll, "what a change it would make! But there's no teacher, no school-room, no nothing, and no prospect of there ever being anything!"

"Why don't you teach 'em yourself?" said Sampson, between the creakings and rasping of his saw.

Noll was silent for a few minutes before he answered, "Why, to tell the truth, I never had thought of the thing. But how can I? I don't have any time till after four o'clock."

The carpenter sawed and planed, and

made no reply, being entirely indifferent to the whole matter; but his chance question had put an idea in Noll's head which was not out of it for that afternoon, at least. Could he teach those idle, ignorant children? he wondered. Would they ever sit still long enough to look in a book? And where could a room for the school be found? And where was the leisure time to come from? Noll pondered over these questions many days, and several times came near discarding the plan as impracticable. He knew that he could only have the time after recitations were over for his own, and that, at the most, would be only an hour or two,—the time between four o'clock and the supper-hour. He was quite sure that he was willing to give this time to the Culm children, if it would do any good, and if a room could be found for them to assemble in. A whole week of days went by before he mentioned this plan to any one, and then it was only Dirk to whom he mentioned it. The rough fisherman looked upon reading and writing as some of the wonderful and mysterious arts to which dull and humble people like himself had no right. He looked blank and mystified at Noll's proposition, and expressed himself thus: —

"I don' know, I don' know, lad, — we but poor folk anyway. But ye ken do as ye like, an' ef ye say so, the youngsters shall take ter books an' sech, an' ye ken hev a room where ye say, I'll say fur't. I don' know, I don' know, lad; ye mus' do as ye think it best, anyway."

CHAPTER XVII.

THE WORK PROGRESSING.

STUDIES at home progressed steadily under Uncle Richard's supervision, meanwhile, and that grim gentleman found much more pleasure and satisfaction in directing his nephew's tasks than he would have been willing to acknowledge. The boy brought so much brightness and pleasant life into the gloomy stone house that the stern master, as week after week passed by, visibly began to lose something of his grimness and gloominess, and to take something like a faint interest in what was passing around him. And, after a time, he himself began to be sensible of this gradual change which was stealing over his thoughts and actions, and, vexed with himself, strove to check these new emotions, and wrap himself again in the cloak of sadness and melancholy which so long had shielded him from everything bright and cheerful and happy. But he found it hardly an easy task. Noll was almost always blithe and light-hearted, and Trafford found his bright influence a hard one to struggle against. He loved the boy so well that it was almost an impossibility to harden his heart to all his winning ways and pleasant talk, which met him so constantly, and these summer days, which Noll found such delight in, were days of struggle and wavering to his uncle. He could not but acknowledge to himself that he was interested in all the boy's plans for the future,—all his youthful anticipations of happiness and success,—all his present little projects for progress and self-improvement,—and these matters, trivial though they may have been, gradually drew his thoughts from himself and his sorrow, put them farther and farther away into the dimness and silence of the past, and made the present a more vivid and earnest reality. Was it any wonder that, seeing he could not maintain his gloom and grimness in Noll's sunshine, and finding it slipping away from him in spite of his endeavors to retain it, he should astonish his nephew by strange fits of moroseness, alternating with the utmost kindness and indulgence?

The boy sometimes fancied that his uncle had grown to utterly dislike him,—being so irritable and unjust at times; then again his heart was light with joy and hope, for he fancied that the grim man was just on the point of losing his great burden of gloom, and becoming hopeful and unoppressed. But how could he be hopeful for whom there was no hope?—who refused to trust in God's promises?—for whom the shadow of the grave was utter darkness and horror, wherein dear faces had vanished—forever?

One day Noll had begged him to come out for a walk on the beach, thinking he would lead his uncle on and on till they should come out upon Culm village, and in this manner disclose what he had been doing for the dwellings and their inmates.

Trafford at first appeared inclined to

consent, and followed his nephew out as far as the piazza steps, but here he stopped, and all Noll's entreaties could not prevail upon him to go further. He sat down, looking dispiritedly across the tranquil sea, all warm and fair with changing lights, and down at his feet at the bit of verdure which Noll had caused to flourish by dint of much seed-sowing and watering, saying, "No, I've no part in it all. I'll go no further."

So Noll was obliged to set off for Culm alone, consoling himself with the thought that next time, perhaps, he should be so successful as to get Uncle Richard a little farther, and next time a little way farther still, till, at last, they might walk together as uncle and nephew should. Would that happy day ever come? he wondered.

At last, after many delays and hindrances, the plan of a school was decided upon. Noll did not begin the undertaking with much confidence of success, or with any great hope of making the Culm children very bright or vigorous scholars; but it would be something toward supplying the great want, he thought, and who could tell what this little beginning might lead to? So, about half-past four one misty, lowery afternoon, he found himself in a little room in Dirk's dwelling, with ten dirty-faced, frowsy-headed children huddled together in one corner, each of them regarding him with wide-open eyes, and apparently without the remotest idea what they were there for. The only furniture which the "schoolroom" could boast were two rough benches, just from John Sampson's hands, and a three-legged stool, which

Noll appropriated to himself. Of course none of the ten had anything in the shape of books or primers, and here the boy had reason to rejoice that all his old school-books had made the journey with himself to Culm.

After getting the wondering assemblage seated in proper order, Noll began by asking, "Who wants to learn to read?"

It seemed as if the sound of his voice had wrought a spell, for each of the ten were as silent as so many mutes.

"Who would like to know how to read?" Noll repeated.

Still a long silence, most discouraging to the teacher. At last — the sound of his voice a most welcome one to Noll — a little fellow, who sat on the end of one of the benches, ventured to query, "What be 'read'?"

"Well," thought the would-be teacher, "I've got to explain what 'read' is before they'll know whether they fancy it, to be sure! I didn't think of that."

Among his books was a great primer, with painted letters and pictures, and bringing this forth, he gathered the ten around him, and used all his powers of description and story-telling to endeavor to awaken the slumbering interest of these unpromising pupils. It was a weary hour's work. A few of them betrayed a slight curiosity in regard to the bright colors, which Noll endeavored to stimulate; but it soon died out, and all looked on and listened with listless attention. They appeared much more inclined to stand with their fingers in their mouths, and gaze steadfastly into Noll's face, than to put eyes on the book.

"If I had the alphabet stamped upon

my face, I believe they'd learn it easily enough!" he thought to himself, in despair, as, on looking up, he found the whole ten staring in his face, instead of having had their eyes upon the primer during his long explanation. As a last resort, he stepped out upon the sand in front of the door, and there drew a great A.

"Now," said he, "see which of you can make a letter like that. Take a stick and try, every one of you. Look sharp, and make it just like the one I've made."

Thereupon, there was a great searching for sticks, and when all the little ones had been supplied, there was a great scratching and marking in the sand. To Noll's great delight, the result was two or three tolerable A's, which were allowed to stand, and the rest were brushed away. Then a new attempt at making the wonderful symbol ensued, and added another to the successful list, and so the letter-making was kept up till all the pupils had succeeded in making a tolerably faithful representation of the letter. Noll began to take heart. What the children cared nothing for, when seen in the book, they were apparently delighted to draw on the sand, and soon learned to give the proper pronunciation of the character. The night came on apace, and Noll began to perceive that it was time for him to be on his homeward way.

"Remember," he said to his pupils, who were scratching A's all about the door, "you're not to forget this while I'm gone. To-morrow afternoon I'll come again, and then I shall want to see you make it over, and you are to have a new letter, besides. Will you all be here?"

"Yes! yes!" one after another promised; and, once more bidding them remember, Noll walked away, — the children still making the mysterious character along the beach, and keeping it up till darkness came over sea and land.

"Only one letter!" Noll said to himself, as he hurried homeward. "Why, that's not a tenth of what I meant to do this afternoon! What dull wits they've got! and will they ever, ever learn the whole alphabet?" The prospect did not seem very encouraging, and he was obliged to confess himself disappointed with the result of the first day's lesson. "However, one can't tell much by the first afternoon," he thought. "Perhaps they'll be quicker and brighter when we're better acquainted."

The next afternoon he arrived at Dirk's house at the appointed time, and found not ten, but twelve awaiting him, sticks in hand, and all eager for the lesson to commence. Noll could not refrain from laughing at the sight which the sand directly in front of the house presented, covered as it was with A's of all shapes and sizes. It looked much as if a great bird, with a peculiarly-constructed foot, had been walking there. He did not need to be assured that his pupils had all remembered yesterday's lesson, and proceeded at once to instruct them in the art of making B. This the young learners of the alphabet found to be somewhat more difficult of execution, but appeared to like it none the less on that account, and, after its curves were mastered, were much delighted with this acquisition to their stock of accomplishments.

While this second lesson was yet in

progress, Dirk and one or two other fishermen came up from their boats, and stopped to look on, with wonder and astonishment written on their countenances.

"I don' know," said Dirk, shaking his head as he eyed the mystic characters traced before him; "we be all poor folk, anyhow, an' this do beat me! Why, what be this?" he exclaimed, pointing at a letter staring up at him from the sand at his feet.

"That be A!" said half a dozen voices at once.

"An' what be this?" said Hark Darby, pointing to a character by his feet.

"That be B!" chorused the voices again.

The two fishermen exchanged wondering glances. "That do beat me!" said poor Dirk, regarding the letters before him with much awe. "Ah, lad," turning to Noll, "my little gal w'u'd liked yer teaching, an' yer B's an' A's, eh?" and Dirk drew his hand across his eyes.

Noll went home much encouraged after this second alphabet lesson. Time and patience would do something for these Culm children, after all, he thought. And could he have the patience and skill which was necessary? "I'll try, — I'll try hard for it!" he thought, "and pray Christ to keep me from losing my patience and courage. It's his work, and he'll help me to teach them, and by winter there'll be something accomplished." And of his help he had great need, for patience and courage were often sorely tried in the days which followed, and it was not always his pupils' obtuseness which brought the greatest strain to bear upon them. One old fish-wife, the oldest woman in the village, had regarded the whole plan of teaching the children as suspicious and ill-omened.

"It be a bad day fur us, lads," she warned, standing on Dirk's door-step among the fishermen, and looking frowningly upon Noll as he instructed his pupils in the making of U. "It be no good fur yer chile to be ther', Hark Darby, learnin' ye don' know what! Yes, lads, I say it be an evil day, and ye'll find no good cum from it! I warn ye, I warn ye!" shaking her skinny forefinger and solemnly nodding her head. Noll's face flushed at these words, and he half resolved to go home, and leave these Culm children to their parents' ignorance.

"I warn ye! I —" The old crone was about to continue her forebodings; but Dirk interposed with a gruff, "Hush ye, hush ye, Mother Deb! ye be doin' the lad wrong. D'ye think he be one to teach our young uns wrong, eh? Be it evil, think ye? W'u'd he be doin' us a bad turn who's mendin' the housen an' makin' us comf'table? I'd like ye ter show't, mother, ef it be!"

"Ay," said Hark Darby, "an' ef he ken do us evil, who ha' been so good an' kind in the sickness, we w'u'd like ye ter show't, Mother Deb!"

The old woman said no more, but went muttering homeward, not all convinced that Noll was not teaching the children some evil, mysterious art.

CHAPTER XVIII.

THE WORK FINISHED.

THE days went by, — busy enough for Noll with lessons and the afternoon lesson at Culm, — and John Sampson's labors began to draw to a close. The carpenter had worked steadily and faithfully, and the result was a gratifying one to more than one person. True, the houses were not models of elegance; that was not needed; and they *did* look somewhat patchy, with here and there a fresh new board over the old weather-beaten gray of the dwelling, and new doors staring blank and yellow out of the dinginess of their surroundings; but, if they were not handsome, they were thoroughly repaired and now stood warmer and more comfortable than any of the present generation of Culm people had ever known them.

If they could only have a coat of paint or whitewash to make them look fresh and cheerful, what an improvement it would be! Noll thought. How the sun would gleam upon them with his last ruddy rays as he sank into the sea! How fair and pleasant they would look from the sea, when the coast first came upon the mariner's vision! It would be one bright spot against the black background of the Rock, —those twelve houses,—if only they might have a coat of fresh white paint. But after counting his stock of money, this desire was obliged to remain ungratified; for there was the carpenter's bill, which would shortly be due, and must be paid upon the completion of the work.

"The houses must wait till—till another year," Noll thought, with something like a sigh; "they can wait, after all, for the painting isn't really necessary, though it would improve them wonderfully! And I'm thankful enough that I can pay the carpenter. Oh, but I wonder if Ned ever regrets his denial, and longs for the pony?"

Letters came down from Ned Thorn with almost every trip of the "Gull," but not a word about the pony did they contain, nor the least sentence which Noll could interpret to mean a sigh or regret for the pet which he had given up. If Ned felt any regret, it was all carefully hidden from his friend's observation, and the missives, which Noll received through the skipper's kindness, were fairly bubbling over with the briskness and bright spirits of Ned's light heart.

"If they should stop coming, I don't know how I *could* manage," thought Noll; "I'm afraid Culm Rock would grow dreadfully lonesome and dreary." It was always, "And how do you get on with your plan?—and are the houses 'most finished?" or, "Have you got those Culm savages almost civilized, you dear old Noll?—and does Uncle Richard know anything about it yet? Won't he stare! and what do you suppose he'll say?" or, "Oh, now I think of it, how many scholars in Latin have you got down there? and how do they manage with their Greek? And are you putting on airs because you've got to be a pedagogue? And how much is the tuition a term? — because, you see, I've some idea of going away to boarding-school, and yours might suit me, if the charges aren't too high." And the whole generally concluded with, "P. S. — I don't mean a word of all that last I've written, my dear Noll, and you're not to think so. How does the money hold out? Don't fail to let me know if you're in a tight place, and I'll try to get a few dollars somehow. And hurry up and answer this letter by return steamer (what should we do if the old 'Gull' went to the bottom?), and so good-night," etc., etc.

Perhaps Noll expected a great deal too much of the Culm people when he looked to see them give up their filthy and slovenly habits at once, after getting fairly settled again in their whole and comfortable abodes. If he really expected to see this, he was disappointed. People do not follow a habit for the best part of a lifetime, to give it up suddenly and at once, even when gratitude and a sense of their short-coming are both urging them to do so. So he was obliged to content himself with some few faint evidences of thrift, and a desire to do better, on the part of those whom he had befriended, and wait patiently for the rest.

Dirk's household improved somewhat. Dirk was the most intelligent of the fishermen, and began to dimly perceive that it was much better and pleasanter to live cleanly and neatly than to pattern his household arrangements after the beasts of the field. He was, moreover, strongly actuated to reform his way of living by his deep, strong sense of gratitude to Noll, which led him to endeavor to accomplish whatever the boy suggested. It gave the stalwart fisherman something like a feeling of shame to see the lad—bright, fresh, and ruddy—enter his dirty and smoke-begrimed hovel and hardly be able to find himself a seat among the litter of old nets, broken chairs, household utensils, and all conceivable kinds of rubbish which strewed the floors and filled the corners.

"It be a shame," Dirk said to his wife, after Noll had gone, one day, "that the lad hev ter stan' up, an' ben't able ter find a seat, nohow. I tell ye it be a shame, woman!"

"Ye might mend the chairs a bit, man!" retorted Mrs. Sharp. "I'll warrant the lad be able ter find a seat then."

Dirk was sulky for a while after this,

but saw that there could be nothing to sit upon so long as the chairs were for the most part legless, and at last got energy enough to mend them after a rude fashion. Then another place was found for the old nets besides the two corners by the fireplace, and when these had been removed, Mrs. Sharp took her broom and — well, it was not exactly sweeping, for the woman had not much idea of what a good housekeeper would call sweeping; but it was a feeble attempt at cleanliness, and she really thought she had made a great exertion, and was certainly proud of the achievement. Dirk chanced to be at home when Noll came again, and the flash of surprise and pleasure which swept over the boy's face as he entered and noted the change which had taken place since his last call pleased Dirk amazingly.

"Here be a seat fur ye, lad," he said, not without some pride in his tone, as he brought forward a rough three-legged block and placed it for his visitor. A faint stir of worthy ambition having slightly roused Dirk and his wife, they were hardly contented to allow matters to remain as they were. Mrs. Sharp once more took her broom, and used it with rather better effect. Dirk made an onslaught upon the rubbish which had been collecting in their kitchen and about the door-steps for years, and which no one had had the energy to remove, and threw many a basketful into the sea.

The neighbors, meanwhile, were not entirely insensible to the fact that Dirk's house began to present — both within and without — a much more cleanly and respectable appearance than their own. They stopped at the door to look in and say, "La, ye be slickin' up finely, Dirk!" or, "Ye be gittin' fine ways, lately, man. An' what be all this fur?"

"Why," Dirk would answer, "I be 'shamed of livin' like a beast, man. An' the young master be wishin' us to hev cleaner housen an' slicker, an' I be willin' to do't ef he wish, now! He be a good lad to mend our housen so finely, and w'u'd ye think I ben't willin' to do his wish?"

Noll was greatly encouraged at these signs of improvement, and mentally rejoiced, hoping to see this new ambition spread till the whole twelve houses were reclaimed from their present filth and wretchedness.

The carpenter's work came to an end at last, — his labor all plain and visible to every eye in patched walls, roofs, mended doors and windows, and the general look of repair about the whole line of what were once but the poorest of shelters. Sampson's task had been a hard and bothersome one,—"Couldn't ha' got another man to teched it," the skipper said,—and Noll expected, as he walked around to Culm one afternoon with his roll of bills to pay the carpenter, that the bill would be a large one,—perhaps even more than Ned's generous bounty and his own amount of spending-money, saved since the lumber was purchased, could meet. He found Sampson packing up his tools,—he was to leave on the "Gull" the next morning,—with the bill all ready, added up and written out on a bit of smooth shingle. It proved to be five dollars less than the sum which Noll held in his hand.

"I swun!" said Sampson, roughly, as he counted over the bills which the boy placed in his hands, "I told the skipper, comin' down, that you was a born fool to be layin' out your money in this style. Now, I've been thinkin' on't over all the while I've been hammerin' and sawin', and I can't make out, to save my neck, how you're goin' to get any return from this 'ere investment. 'Tain't payin' property, I should judge," said the carpenter, looking up and down the beach.

"Of course I don't expect to get any money back from it," said Noll, laughing a little at the idea. "It was to help these fish-folk and to try and make them more comfortable that I did it."

Sampson put the roll of bills away in his capacious purse, remarking, "Well, you're a queer un. I did the job right well, though, if I do say it, and I ha'n't charged very steep for it, neither. Couldn't do it, somehow! — went too much against the grain. And — well, can't you shake hands over it? You're a tip-top paymaster, and if you want anything done, I'll come and do it, if I'm in China — there! Don't you lay out another cent on this settlement, though, — 'tain't worth it."

Noll did not promise to take this advice, and started homeward, Sampson calling after him, "Good-by, good-by, lad! Hope you'll get some return from this 'ere investment!"

So the work was done, and a glad and happy letter went over the sea to Hastings, telling Ned Thorn that the labor was accomplished, and the houses all as whole and comfortable as when new, and that the people were actually beginning to show a little thrift and ambition; and saying, among other things, "I send you back five dollars that were left, — so you can begin to save your money again for that pony. And, oh! Ned, I don't think you can know how much good that money did! Perhaps you never will know (it must seem to you almost like throwing it away, because you are where you cannot see any result from it), and I felt, at first, as if you ought not to make the denial; but, somehow, I'm very glad, now, and I shall always feel sure that if you *do* make fun and pretend to laugh at a plan, you're all the time meaning to 'give it a lift,' as you say. And, oh! Ned, I believe I'm one of the happiest boys in the world! and I'm sure Uncle Richard has changed a great deal since last spring, when you were here, for he's got over being cross and gloomy, and actually asked me yesterday where I spent so much of my time. I'm going, if I can, to persuade him to take a walk with me, one of these afternoons, and so bring him around to the new houses. Wouldn't you like to be here to see us then? As for my school, it flourishes a little. There are still twelve scholars, and all but four have got through with their sand letters, and are at work at their 'a–b, ab,' and 'b–a, ba.' They'll get into spelling-books, sometime. Now, I'll end this long letter with telling you once more that you can't know how much good your money has done and will do, and say, Good-night,

"NOLL TRAFFORD."

Noll did not lose sight for a moment of his plan to persuade Uncle Richard to take a walk with him. It filled his thoughts all the pleasant days that followed after Mr. Sampson's departure, and several times he hinted very broadly to his uncle that it was "a splendid afternoon for a walk! the beach is hard as a floor, and the tide out." But Trafford was oblivious to all hints, and at last, on one warm, balmy, cloudless afternoon, Noll thought, "It is now, or never! I'll ask him at once." And straightway he started for the library, where he knew his uncle sat reading.

CHAPTER XIX.

A HAPPY WALK.

TRAFFORD looked up from his books as his nephew entered, and greeted him with a smile. Noll thought this welcome portended good, and remembered, with a grateful thrill in his heart, that Uncle Richard had fallen into the habit of greeting him thus of late. He went up to the reader's chair, and without waiting for his courage to cool, laid a hand on the reader's arm, saying, —

"Uncle Richard, I've come to ask a great favor of you. Do you think you'll grant it? Can't you guess what it is?"

Trafford did not reply at once, but sat looking steadfastly into his nephew's face, his eyes wearing the dreamy, far-away look which lingered in them much of late, and it was not until Noll had repeated his question that he replied, musingly,—

"I'm sure I cannot think. Perhaps you wish more pocket-money, or—"

"Oh, no!" answered the boy, quickly, "it's nothing like that, Uncle Richard! It's—it's—oh, it's will you take a walk?"

Trafford's forehead began to wrinkle and slowly gather the shade of gloom which seemed alway hovering about him, even in his most cheerful moments; but before it had time to cover the man's brow, and before he could utter a refusal, Noll's hand was endeavoring to smooth away the wrinkles, and he was saying,—

"There, don't say 'No,'—don't, Uncle Richard! I won't ask you to go again if you are not pleased with this walk, but *this* time—just *this* once—do say 'Yes,' uncle! There can't be a pleasanter afternoon in the whole year than this, and I've walked alone, always till now. Why, Uncle Richard, you won't say 'No' *this* time?"

Trafford hesitated, a refusal trembling on his lips, which he did not quite wish to utter. The boy *had* walked alone, he remembered, and it was a very simple request to grant; and if it was going to be such a pleasure and gratification to Noll, why not yield, and for once put aside his own preferences and inclinations? It is not an easy matter for a man who has lived only for himself and his own pleasure to put the gratification of these aside to give place to the happiness and comfort of another; but, with an effort, Trafford put his books away, and rose from his chair, saying, —

"This once, Noll, — this once. One walk with me will suffice you, I think. When shall we start?"

"Now, — at once, Uncle Richard!" said Noll, joyfully; "it's two o'clock already, and the tide a long, long way out. Don't let's wait a minute longer."

Trafford smiled a little at his nephew's eagerness, and taking his hat, followed the boy to the piazza. It was a great change from the half-gloom of the library, and the chilliness of the long, dark halls, to the bright, sunny piazza, where the light fell so warm and broadly, and from whence the blue and shining sea stretched far and wide and vast.

Noll felt sure that Uncle Richard must notice it and rejoice, even though it might be secretly. From east to west there were no clouds, and nothing to hinder the sunbeams from finding the earth and working wondrous charms on land and rock and sea. They stood for a few minutes there, one of them, at least, enjoying the wide view very much, then Noll said,—

"We'll go up the shore, if you'd as lief, Uncle Richard. It's much pleasanter that way, I think."

"Very well," said Trafford, with an indifference which was not encouraging, and they passed down the steps on to the sand. It was a silent and uncomfortable walk for the first few rods, Trafford walking with his head bowed upon his breast and looking only at the yellow sand upon which he trod. He seemed to have no eyes for the calm and gentle peace which had descended upon that afternoon, robbing the sea of its terror and making it enchanting and lovely, and weaving a mystic charm about the bare, bald Rock basking warm and purple under the sun. Even the waves murmured only softly and soothingly and with drowsy echoes, as they rippled in and out among the rocks and along the sand. Fortunately for their pleasure, Noll picked up a curious pebble before they had gone a great way. It was not an agate, nor was it like the rounded pebbles of porphyry which the tide washed up, and puzzling over this, and asking Uncle Richard, at last, to explain its nature, somehow broke the heavy silence which had been between them, and questions and pleasant talk came naturally enough after this.

Trafford lost his gloom and reserve, and followed after his nephew, chatting and explaining strange matters of rock and sea, and stopping now and then to pull over great bunches of freshly-stranded kelp to help Noll search for rare shells or bits of scarlet or purple weed which were hidden and entangled there. How brightly shone the sun! What peace and calm hovered over land and sea! He was just beginning to be conscious of the joy and loveliness which the afternoon held. It was no wonder, he thought, that Noll's blithe, unclouded heart loved such a pleasant earth, and found delight in all the hours which flitted by. But for himself, alas! all this brightness was clouded over by the ever-present, ever-shadowing darkness of the future. It might have been different if— if— But with a sigh Trafford put away these thoughts, and followed on. They lingered around the rocks in their path, black with fringes of dry sea-weed, and talked of gneiss and sienite, granite and trap; they stopped at the curve in the shore, and sat down to watch the white flitting of sails on the far horizon-line, and somehow, the sight of them led to a long talk about Hastings and Noll's papa, and happy memories of other days. Trafford was in a softened mood as they rose up from their seat on a great fragment which had fallen from the cliff above, and Noll said,—

"Come, Uncle Richard, let's keep on toward Culm. It's *so* pleasant, and night is a long way off yet."

If he had followed his own inclinations,

the uncle would have turned about and retraced his steps, but Noll had started on, and Trafford followed, thinking, "It isn't often the boy has company in his rambles. I can humor him for once."

Slowly enough they approached the Culm houses, loitering along the moist, shining sand, over which the waves had rolled and rippled but a few hours before, and marking their devious path with straying footprints. Noll's heart began to beat somewhat faster as they neared the fishermen's houses, and he kept a keen watch upon his uncle's face in order to detect the first look of surprise and astonishment that should come across it when he perceived how the huts had been improved. But Trafford's eyes were turned toward the sea, thoughtfully and gravely, and they drew very near the village without the discovery being made. They came upon Dirk, Hark Darby, and two or three other fishermen, spreading their nets in the sun, all of whom touched their hats and nodded respectfully to Noll, eying the uncle, meanwhile, with curious eyes and half-averted faces. The sight of these men brought Trafford's eyes and thoughts back to Culm and the present. He turned to Noll, saying, with a little smile,—

"Some of your sworn friends?"

"Yes, they're my friends, Uncle Richard," said Noll, expecting every moment to see Trafford raise his eyes to the houses, which they were passing, "and they do me a great many favors too."

"In what way?" Trafford was about to ask; but just then he looked up and about him, and the words died on his lips. Noll paused, waiting in suspense for what was to come next. His uncle stood still, and looked for a full minute upon Dirk's house, then cast his eyes up and down the line of dwellings, while a look of wonder and amazement came over his face. He turned about, and looked at Noll, who could not, for the life of him, keep the bright color from creeping up into his cheeks and over his forehead, and then he looked at the houses again. A sudden suspicion came into Trafford's mind, and turning his keen eyes upon Noll, he exclaimed,—

"Can you explain this?"

The nephew hesitated, looked down in some embarrassment, then gathering sudden courage, looked up and answered, brightly, "Yes, Uncle Richard, I know all about it."

It was all plain to Trafford then. For a moment his own eyes faltered and refused to meet Noll's, and he showed some signs of emotion. But his voice and tone were as calm as ever when he said, a few minutes after,—

"*You* did this? How can I believe it? What had you to do with? And why was I not consulted, if this was your work?"

"Oh, Uncle Richard!" said Noll, quickly, "don't be vexed with me. You gave me permission to help these Culm people. Don't you remember?"

Trafford made no reply, and again looked at the line of comfortable, well-repaired houses. There were deeper thoughts and emotions in his heart at that moment than Noll could know or guess.

The long silence was so uncomfortable that the boy was fain to break it, with, "I've one more thing to show you, Uncle Richard. It's not much,—only just a beginning, — but I'd like you to see and know about it."

Trafford followed, without a word, and Noll led the way to the little schoolroom, with its two benches and three-legged stool and pile of well-thumbed primers and spelling-books.

"It's not much," said Noll, apologetically, "but it's a beginning, and they all know their letters, and some can spell a little."

Trafford evinced no surprise, much to Noll's wonder, and merely asked, "Where do you find the time?"

"After recitations," replied the nephew; and that was all that was said about the matter.

Trafford went out and sat down on the little wharf, and Noll lingered in the doorway of his schoolroom, thinking that he had never seen Uncle Richard act more strangely. Was he offended at what he had done and was doing for the Culm people? he wondered. He looked out and saw that his uncle had turned his face away, and was looking off upon the sea with the same dreamy, thoughtful look which he had noticed in his eyes of late. Noll would have given a great deal could he have known his thoughts at that moment. To human eyes this grave and thoughtful man, who sat on the wharf, was not a whit less the stern and gloomy creature that he had been an hour before. Yet, all hidden from others' gaze, and almost from his own consciousness, a sudden sense of regret and of a great shortcoming in himself had welled up through the crust of his hardened heart. His heart had been deeply stirred, and now it smote him. His thoughts took some such shape as this, — even while he was looking with such apparent calmness upon the changing, shadowy lights of the sea: —

"This boy has done more in this short summer for his fellow-men and for his God than I have done in my whole forty years of life! Oh, what a life mine has been! — all a wreck, a failure, a miserable waste! And he? Why, in this short summer-time, and on this barren Rock, he has made his very life a blessing to every one upon it. I suppose those dirty, ignorant fishermen bless the day that brought him here. And I? O Heaven! what a failure, what a failure! I've done the world no good, — it's no better for my having lived in it, — it would miss me no more than one of these useless pebbles which I cast into the sea. And this boy — *my* boy — always at work to make others rejoice that he was born into the world!"

For all the calmness and repose that was on his face, he longed to cry out. Oh! was there no deliverance? Might not these long wasted years yet be paid for by deeds of mercy and charity? But where was there a deliverer? and who could tell how many years of good deeds and charity could pay for forty years of wasted ones?

CHAPTER XX.

NEW THOUGHTS AND NEW PLANS.

NOLL, sitting in the doorway, was presently aroused from a little reverie into which he had fallen by hearing a voice call, "Noll, my boy, come here."

He obeyed the call, and started for the little wharf, half expecting that Uncle Richard was about to reprove him for what he had done. Trafford gazed in his nephew's face for a short space, and then, smothering what his heart longed to cry out, and what he had intended to say to the boy, he sighed only, "We will start homeward, if you are ready."

Noll was sure that his uncle had kept back something which it was in his heart to say, and, wondering what it could be, he followed after the tall figure along the homeward path.

The sun was getting well down into the west. The fair clearness of the sky was broken by a soft, mellow haze which began to steal across it, yet the afternoon was no less beautiful, and along the horizon there were long and lovely trails of misty color, — faint, delicate flushes of amber and purple, — which gave an added charm to the day's declining.

Not a word did uncle and nephew speak till, as they rounded the curve of the shore, and the stone house came in sight, Trafford asked, abruptly, "Noll, where did your pocket-money go?"

The boy explained the whole matter, with an account of Ned Thorn's bounty and help, at the last, and then they paced along the sand in silence, as before. Noll managed to get many looks at his uncle's face, and seeing that it wore no stern nor forbidding aspect, ventured to ask, —

"Are you offended with me, or what, Uncle Richard?"

Trafford took his nephew's hand as he replied, "Not in the least, Noll."

His voice was strangely kind and tender, and Noll exclaimed, looking up joyfully and brightly, "I'm very glad, Uncle Richard! and do you know your voice sounded like papa's just now?"

They walked hand in hand along the

shore, — Noll, at least, very happy, — and looking afar at the sea through glad and hopeful eyes. He mentally prayed that Uncle Richard's gloom and sternness might never return, and that he might always be in his present softened and subdued mood. They came to the stone house at last, and, as they reached the steps, Noll took one long look at his uncle's face, thinking to himself that not soon again should he see it so gentle and tender, for the gloom of the library would soon shadow it, and make it once more stern and forbidding. But, just as if he felt something of this himself, Trafford lingered on the steps, as if loath to go in, and at last sat down. Noll inwardly rejoiced, and seated himself on the bit of green which he had caused to grow, by much watering and nourishing, close beside the piazza. That little breadth of grass, with its deep verdure, was a wonderfully pleasant thing for the eyes to rest upon in this waste of rock and sand. Trafford looked down at it and at the boy sitting there,—his curly locks blown all about his face by the warm wind, —and thought to himself, that, wherever the lad went, brightness and pleasantness sprang up about him, even though the soil was naught but sand and barrenness. His heart was full of reproachful cries. "What this boy has done,—and *I!*" was a thought continually haunting him. And he did not try to put it away; but, as he sat there, went back over all the months of the lad's stay, remembering what he had done to brighten the old stone house and himself, and contrasting all the boy's actions and motives with his own,—sparing himself not at all in the condemnation which his own heart was ready to pronounce. "What this boy has done, — and *I!* I? Nothing, nothing! The earth will never miss me, for I have had no part in its life, and have cared naught for its joys or its sorrows; and beyond — where this boy's heaven lies — there will be no place for me, because I have not sought it, and have cared only for my own peace. So I have no part nor place in the world or out of it." A more vivid sense of this truth came to Trafford here, and he sighed long and heavily, thinking of what might have been. He saw and felt what a great matter it was to have a heart wherein God's love dwelt so steadfastly that eye nor ear could ever be closed against the wants of his creatures, and the work of his that lay waiting for the doing. And it was another matter to have a heart so cold and frozen that no warmth of his love ever thrilled it with pity or compassion, — ever drew it with tender, gentle guidance toward himself, — ever stirred it with longings for his love and his blessing and upholding. It was no wonder, he thought, that for one heart the earth was joyous and beautiful, while for the other it was but a gloomy, unhappy waste; for over the pure, warm heart's earth God reigned, and his sunshine lighted it, and his flowers blossomed by the wayside, and they who lived in the land were his own, and their needs the needs of his children. All doing was but doing for God, while in a cold, frozen heart his work is not remembered, and the sunshine is but gloom, because it does not come from him, and the flowers are not his, and the poor soul mourns and sorrows, wrapped up in its own darkness and chilliness, and fails to find the earth bright or beautiful.

With such thoughts as these in his heart, Trafford was silent a long time. The sun set, and shadows began to steal over the sea, gradually and softly wrapping its farther distances in hazy indistinctness. Hagar's voice, from the kitchen-door, where she was calling her chickens to their supper, floated around to his ears and awoke him from his long and sorrowful reverie. He started up, surprised to see how fast the light had flitted from sky and earth. Noll still sat on the bit of grass, busy over a heap of shells and pebbles, which he had gathered during his afternoon walk. Trafford looked at him a few minutes in silence, and finally asked,—

"What plans have you made for winter about your school, my boy?"

A sudden look of surprise flitted over the boy's face ere he answered, "I haven't made any, Uncle Richard. I can't, you see, because the days will be so short that I'm afraid there'll not be time after my recitations. And there's no stove nor fireplace in the room, and not much of anything comfortable. But I'm going to try, though," he added, hopefully.

Trafford was silent and thoughtful for a long time. At last he said, "What would you say if I forbade you to continue your school through the winter?"

"I don't think you'll say that, Uncle Richard," said Noll,—not very confidently, however. "I should be very sorry to give it up now."

"Even if I thought it best?"

Noll could not deny but that he should. "They're just beginning to learn," he said,

Culm Rock.

"and it would be too bad for them to lose all they have gained. Don't you really think so, too, Uncle Richard?"

Trafford made no reply to this question, but, when he spoke again, said, "Not even if another teacher filled your place, Noll?"

The boy's tongue was silent with wonder and astonishment. Then, thinking his ears had deceived him, he said, "Why—why—what did you say, Uncle Richard?"

"I asked you," said Trafford, "whether you would be willing to give up the school if another teacher took your place?"

The warm, eager color rushed into Noll's face, and he cried, "Do you mean that—that—a teacher might take my place, Uncle Richard? Do you really mean it? Were you in earnest, and shall I answer?"

"To be sure," said his uncle, gravely enough.

"Oh, Uncle Richard!" cried Noll, "I *knew* the time would come some day! I knew it! I knew it! And will you hire a teacher for those Culm children? Was that what you meant?"

"I do not know that they need two," said Trafford.

"Yes, I'll give up the school this minute!" said Noll, remembering that he had not answered his uncle's question; "I'm willing to, if the children can only have a teacher. Oh, but it seems too good to be true! And are you really going to hire some one to take my place?"

"I have hardly thought yet; you must not press questions upon me too fast. I do not know my own mind."

Hagar heard their voices, and came around the piazza corner to say, "Tea hab been waitin' fur ye dis yer whole hour, Mas'r Dick, an' 'tain't growin' better, nohow. Will ye hab it wait any longer?"

"No, we're coming, shortly," said Trafford, and presently they went in to tea, for which Noll had not the least appetite, in spite of his long walk,—it being quite driven away by the question which his uncle had put to him,—and he spent most of the meal-time in taking keen and watchful looks at Uncle Richard's face, to see when it began to cloud over with gloom and grow stern and moody again. But the shadow which he so much dreaded did not make its appearance, and from the supper-table they went to the library, where Hagar had lit the lamp, Noll feeling wonderfully happy and quite sure that this was the eve of a brighter day for Uncle Richard and the Culm people.

Contrary to his usual habit, Trafford did

not take up his books on reaching the library, but sat looking thoughtfully at Noll, and at last, as if speaking his thoughts aloud, he said,—

"If a new teacher comes, a new schoolroom will have to follow, as a matter of consequence; and those two rough benches which I saw over at Culm are hardly the best style of school furniture. And how is it about books?"

"There are none but primers and leaves from old spelling-books," said Noll, sitting very still and quiet with delight at hearing Uncle Richard ask such questions. It all seemed like a dream, and not at all a matter of reality. What could have come across the man's feelings so suddenly and with such effect?

Trafford resumed his inquiries after a short silence, and little by little drew from his nephew the whole story of the school's commencement, and what drawbacks the lack of a good room, with seats and desks and the necessary books, were, till he had made himself acquainted with all the needs of the school. He talked with Noll about the Culm people, and listened to the boy's hopeful and enthusiastic account of their slight improvement, with something that was very like interest. But the school seemed to interest him most. He proposed that a teacher be sent for to take charge of the school during the winter, and that the best room which could be found among the houses be fitted up as a schoolroom, and as nicely and warmly as possible. The teacher and the furniture would have to come from Hastings, and most likely a carpenter would be needed. Noll thought of John Sampson at once.

So the evening passed away in planning and discussion, and when Noll went to bed, it seemed as if all the events of the afternoon and evening were but phases of a happy dream, which morning light would banish as unreal. His thankfulness for this token of dawn, after the long, black, weary night of gloom through which he had struggled, could not find words enough in which to praise God for this promise of brighter days. He prayed that it might not be fleeting, and that morning might not show this gleam of brightness to be only imaginary. But the morrow came, and proved yesterday's events to be real and true, and Uncle Richard still without his stern and gloomy face, and ready to perfect the plans which they had discussed the previous evening.

One day after another passed, till Noll

began to be certain that Uncle Richard's gloom and moroseness had departed from him forever. The boy wondered and surmised, but could not account for this sudden disappearance of the shadow. What had wrought the change so suddenly? Would it last alway? True, Uncle Richard was not cheerful yet, and he seemed to be carrying some heavy grief or sorrow about with him; but from his face the grimness and gloominess were gone, and Noll was sure that there must be some little change in his heart, else he would not care for the welfare of these Culm children.

A week or two elapsed before this new plan was put in operation, or rather before anything was done toward carrying it out. The skipper was hardly the person to intrust with the care of finding a teacher and looking up school-books, and for a time they were in doubt and perplexity. Then Noll proposed—what he had long been wishing—to go to Hastings himself, and find such a teacher as was needed, procure the suitable books and furniture, and bring John Sampson back with him. It would require but a week's absence, and in that time all the business could be done, and some happy days be spent with Ned Thorn and old friends.

Trafford hesitated a long time. Who could tell what peril the boy might be in while crossing the sea? How could he lose him now? And, when once in the charmed circle of old friends and associations, would he not dislike to return to gray and barren Culm Rock? But Noll went.

CHAPTER XXI.

IN PERIL OF THE SEA.

THE day had dawned clear and brilliant, but as the afternoon waned, a gray curtain of ragged cloud slowly rose and hid the sun, and brought an early nightfall. The wind was strong, and the sea — calm and silvery but a few hours before — began to toss and thunder heavily. Hagar came from the pine woods with a great basket of cones, just as the early dusk began to settle over the windy sea and to wrap the forest in heavy shadow, and as the old woman crossed the narrow bar of sand which connected Culm Rock with the main-land, the wind swept over in such strong gusts, and with such blinding sheets of spray, that her safety was more than once endangered. But she reached the firm, unyielding Rock, with no worse misfortune than a drenching befalling her, and made her way to the warm and comfortable precincts of her kitchen, with many ejaculations of delight and thankfulness. The first sound which greeted her ears on entering was the long-drawn, solemn voice of the organ.

"Wonder what Mas'r Dick's got on his heart dis yer night?" she muttered, bustling about to prepare supper; "'tain't sech music as dat yer organ make lately. 'Pears like somethin' was de matter, anyhow."

She prepared supper in the dining-room, muttering to herself about the lonesomeness and silence of the house since "Mas'r Noll dun gone off;" and when the solitary meal was in readiness, put her head in at the library-door and called her master to tea. When she had got back to her kitchen, and was standing in the open door, her grizzled head thrust out into the gathering gloom and tempest to watch the progress of the storm, she noticed that the music did not cease, but kept on in its slow and solemn measure, rising and falling and stealing plaintively in.

"Somethin's de matter, sure," Hagar said, turning about and shutting the door; "dat ain't de kind of music dat Mas'r Dick's made lately. 'Pears like he's 'stressed 'bout somethin'! But, Hagar, ye can't do nuffin but jes' trust de Lord, nohow. Ye'd better get yer own supper, ef yer Mas'r Dick don't tech his."

She ate her supper and washed the dishes, and gave the little kitchen a stroke or two with her broom, and yet the music from the library came stealing in as sad-voiced and heavy as ever.

"'Pears as if he'd never eat his supper," Hagar grumbled; "de chile can't live on music, allers, nohow. Reckon he'll nebber hab much sperits till he eats more. But jes' stop yer talkin', chile, ye can't do nuffin' but trust de Lord."

By and by the wandering notes ceased, and in the deep silence there came up the hoarse and awful roar of the surf, with the wailing of the wind over the chimney, and filled the house with their echoes. Hagar heaped wood on the fire, drew her little low chair nearer the light and gladsome blaze, shivering and muttering as she did so. She had a great dread of cold and darkness, and the deep hush, broken by the clamor of the sea, made her afraid.

"De Lord's about," said she, drawing her old woollen shawl close around her; "de Lord's on de sea, an' 'pears like nobody need be feared when he holds it in his hand like as I holds dis yer silber ob Mas'r Noll's dat he lost under de rug in de dinin'-room,"—looking down at the shining coin which she had picked up that morning, and wondering where the boy was at that moment. "'Pears as ef de sunshine had been hid de whole time sence he went off to de city," she muttered, gazing in the coals. "Wonder ef Mas'r Dick misses him? Wonder ef dis yer ole woman won't be tickled 'nuff to see him when de day comes? Ki! Hagar, ye knows ye will."

The roar of the sea and the cry of the wind came in again, more lonesome, sadder than ever. The old negress shivered, peered about her into the dark corners of the kitchen, and crooned to herself,— a wild, monotonous air, set to words which came to her lips for the occasion:—

"Oh, Hagar, don't ye know
De Lord's on de sea?
He rides on de waves,
And de wind is in his hand,—
De Lord keeps dem all!

What ye feared of, Hagar? Kase, don't ye know de Lord's in it? 'Pears like ye done forget dat de whole time—Now!" and she broke into her rhymeless chant again. It was only a way she had got of setting her thoughts to music, drawing the words out very slowly, and weaving to and fro the while. When she had repeated her first lines, she kept on with her thoughts, peering over her shoulder at the flickering shadows which the fire cast on the wall behind her, shivering with awe at the clamor without, and chanting, waveringly,—

"Oh, Hagar, don't ye know
De Lord's on de sea?
De wind blows, an' de sky is dark,
An' de sea *cries like a little chile,*
An' de boats will be blowed away;
But de Lord is good, an' mornin' will come,
An', oh, Hagar, sing hallelujah!
Fur de Lord is in it all!"

Here she stopped her chanting, and began to sing "Hallelujah!" softly, ceasing her swaying, to look into the coals. The fire burned down to rosy embers, in which little blue-tongued flames darted up fitfully, —anon lighting up the room brilliantly, then dying away and leaving it almost in darkness, — while Hagar's crooning died away to a whisper. A little gray light still shone in at the kitchen-window, but it was fast flitting. The roar of the sea became thunder, the wind grew tempestuous. By and by the rain began to fall, sounding strangely soft and still, when compared with the din of wind and waves.

"God bress us!" said Hagar, "dis yer is an awful night. Keep de boats off de Rock, Lord, and pity de sailors in dis yer awful storm!"

The old woman knew how the sea must look now, —yeasty, horrible, its white wave-caps shining through the darkness and hurrying to topple over and thunder against the rocks. To her, as she sat crouched before the fire, it seemed to howl and scream and mourn hoarsely, like some great voice rending the night with lamentation.

"Call on de Lord, Hagar," she muttered frequently; "can't nuffin else help ye now!"

Sometimes she fell to chanting her thoughts, — the sound of her own voice was pleasant to her in the loneliness, — and she piled cedar chips on the fire to see their cheerful blaze and enjoy their brisk crackle.

"Might as well hab a candle," she said, after a time. "Git yer knittin', chile, an' 'pear as ef ye didn't distrus' de Lord. What ef de wind is blowin'? what ef de sea is a-screamin'? Don't ye know whose wind and whose sea 'tis?" She got up to grope for a candle on the shelf over the fireplace.

"Hagar!" exclaimed a voice at the farther end of the kitchen, — a voice so full of compressed fear and anxiety that the old negress tumbled back in her chair with affright, — "Hagar! are you here?" demanded the voice.

"Bress ye! yes, I's here, Mas'r Dick!" she answered, catching sight of his white face by the dining-room door. "I's here, but ye spoke so suddent! Jes' wait, an' I'll hab a candle in a minnit."

The candle was found, and, after a long blowing of coals and burning of splinters, began to burn dimly. Hagar set it on the table, and looked up at her master with a start of alarm, his face was so white and anxious.

"Hagar," said he, huskily, "*Noll was to start from Hastings this morning!*"

The old negress stood looking at him a full minute, — a fearful, lonesome minute in which the rain beat against the panes, and the awful voice of the sea filled the room,—then she sank down by the fire with a low cry.

"Lord bress us all!" she wailed, as she looked up, "fur he'll nebber get here, Mas'r Dick!"

Trafford looked at her silently. Oh, that awful voice without!—the thunder, the tremble of the earth, the screaming of the wind! At last,—

"Is ye certain sure, Mas'r Dick? D'ye *know* he started? Did he say?"

"Oh, Hagar, if I did not—*not know*,—if I had any doubt that he started, I would give all my possessions this very moment!"

"'Tain't de money nor de lands dat'll do now!" moaned Hagar, beginning to sway back and forth; "it's only de Lord! De Lord's on de sea to-night, an' 'tain't fur man to say! Oh, Mas'r Dick! t'ink o' dat bressed boy in dese waves an' dis wind!"

"Hush!" said the master, imperatively, "I will *not* think of it! It can't be! Noll? Oh, Hagar, I believe I'm going mad!" He turned away from the old negress and opened the door. The tempest swept in, overturning the candle and flaring up the fire, and bearing the rain, in one long gust, across the little kitchen, even into Hagar's face.

Trafford stood there, regardless of wind and rain, looking out upon the sea. The mighty tumult awed him and filled his heart with a sense of man's utter weakness and helplessness. The foamy expanse gleamed whitely through the night,—awful with the terror of death,—and its deafening roar smote upon his ears, and in the slightest lull, the rain-drops fell with a soft, dull patter. Noll in it all?—in this fearful, yawning sea,—in this wild tumult of wind and rain,—in the vast waste of waves which the thick darkness shrouded, and where death was riding? "God help me!" he cried in sudden frenzy,—"God help me!" He looked up at the thick, black depths of sky with a groan of agony when he remembered his utter powerlessness. But what right had he to look to Heaven for aid?—he who knew not God, nor sought him, nor desired his love? The bitterness of this thought made him groan and beat his breast. Would He—whom all his life long he had refused and rejected—hear his cries?

Hagar's voice came to him here through all the din and thunder, beseeching that the door might be closed. He closed it behind him, and stepped out into the darkness. It was already past the hour for the "Gull" to arrive, he remembered, and then a sudden thought flashed through his brain that beacons ought to be kindled to guide the skipper, if he were not already beyond the need of earthly guides and beacons. And close upon this thought came a remembrance of the Culm fishermen,—stout, skilful sailors, all of them,—and a great hope filled his heart that in them he might find aid in his extremity. And without waiting for a second thought, he started through the inky darkness and the tempest for Culm village. He ran till he was breathless. He climbed and groped his way over and along the slippery rocks, the awful voice of the sea filling his ears and goading him on.

CHAPTER XXII.

WEARY WATCHING.

THE evening wore on. They were all on the beach,— Trafford and the Culm fishermen,—and now a beacon fire streamed up into the darkness, and made the night seem even more black and intense. They had piled their heap of driftwood somewhat in the shelter of a great rock, and around it the men were huddled, muttering and whispering to each other, and casting sober glances at Trafford, who stood apart from them in the shadow. Not a word had he spoken since the fire was kindled, but, grim and silent as a statue, had stood there, with his eyes looking upon the gleaming sea, and the rain beating in his face. He had worked desperately while gathering drift-wood.

"The master be crazed, like," Dirk had whispered to the men as they came in with armfuls of fuel. "D'ye see his eyes? D'ye see the way he be runnin' up an' down, poor man?"

"Ay, an' his lad be where many o' your'n an' mine ha' been, eh, Dirk?" said Hark Harby. "Mabby he ken tell what 'tis ter be losin' his own, an' no help fur it, eh?"

"'Sh!" said Dirk; "the sea ben't able

ter get sech a lad as his every day. If he be lost, 'tis a losin' fur more'n he, yender."

This was before the beacon was kindled. Now they huddled in a gloomy circle about the hissing, sputtering fire, some crouching close to the rock to save themselves from the rain, and the others drawing their heads down into their wide-collared jackets, that bade defiance to the wet. The wind whirled and raved, and the sea thundered on. The fire cast a little pathway of light through the darkness, down to the sea's edge, and they could see its waves all beaten to foam as white as milk, flecking the sand in great patches. It was an awful waiting.

By and by Hagar came down along the sand in a great hood-cloak that gave her a most weird and witchlike appearance.

The fishermen looked at her with startled, suspicious eyes as the bent old figure suddenly emerged from the darkness into the full glare of the firelight. The old negress passed on to where Trafford was standing.

"I's here, Mas'r Dick," she said, touching his arm, as if fain to assure him of her presence and sympathy.

He did not repel her, but said, with much of kindness in his tone, "This is no place for you, Hagar."

"De Lord's here," said Hagar, quietly, "an' I's gwine ter stay. I isn't feared, Mas'r Dick."

Trafford looked in her wrinkled, time-worn old face yearningly. This black, ignorant old woman had something within her heart that gave her a peace and serenity in this fearful hour that he envied. He felt the truth of this as he had never felt it before. She was stayed and upheld by some invisible hand. Somehow, in her humble life, this old negress had found some great truth which all his own study and research had failed to teach him. He turned about and made her a seat of boards on an old spar which lay on the sand, under the shelter of the rock by the fire.

"T'ank ye, Mas'r Dick," said Hagar, tremulously, as she sat down. This unusual kindness touched her. It was like his old-time thoughtfulness and gentleness, when he was her own blithe, merry schoolboy, she thought.

The rain began to fall less heavily. Only now and then a great drop fell with a hiss and sputter into the fire; but the wind grew fiercer as the evening waned, and the thunder and pounding of the sea was deafening. The spray dashed higher and higher, quite up to the backs of the men who huddled about the fire, and its fine mist sifted even into Hagar's face and grizzled locks.

"'Tain't nuffin tu what dat bressed boy is suff'rin'," she sighed, wiping the cold drops off her cheeks; "'pears as ef dis ole heart 'ud split'n two, thinkin' ob it. O good Lord, bress de chile!—bress him,—bress him!—dat's all Hagar ken say."

It was a weary watching. As the war of the sea grew louder and the wind fiercer, the Culm fishermen gathered into a yet closer group, and looked with awed and sober faces in the fire. For all that these men followed the sea, and it was almost a native element to them, they seemed to have a great dread and awe of it. Trafford yet stood apart from them with his eyes looking into the dense night, and Hagar, all muffled in her great cloak, swayed slowly to and fro with her face hidden. Oh, the suspense and agony of those minutes!—the weary watching and waiting for—what?

It came at last. In the short space of silence between the bursting of two great waves, there rose a cry from out the great waste of darkness beyond their little length and breadth of light. Trafford started and sprang forward. The men around the fire were startled from their crouching positions by this shrill, sudden shout, and looked in one another's faces and—waited. But the cry was not repeated. Then Dirk said,—

"It wur the skipper, sure. O Lord, men! but I be feared the 'Gull' be on the rocks, yender."

The sweat stood in drops on his forehead, and he slowly clinched and unclinched his great brawny hands. Trafford heard his words, and a sudden faintness like death smote him. But it passed away, and in sudden frenzy and despair he rushed up to Dirk, exclaiming,—

"How do you know, man? How can you tell? There was only a cry!"

Before Dirk could answer, there rose, clear and distinct, that one solitary voice from out the darkness,—a fearful, appealing cry for aid from some human heart out there in the awful presence of death. And that thrilling cry was all. It never came again. Trafford beat his breast with agony. Then he turned upon the fishermen.

"Why do you stand here," he cried, furiously, "when they are perishing out there? My boy is there!—my boy that's done so much for you and yours! Will you let him drown without lifting a hand to save him?"

"It be no use to try," said the men, pointing to the surf; "boat's ud crack like a gull's shell out there."

"But try,—only try!" shouted Trafford, in an agonized tone. "If money will tempt you, you shall have all of mine! You shall have more than ever your eyes saw before! I will make you all rich!—only try,—only try!"

"We'd try soon enough for the young master's sake, an' ye might keep yer gold," said Dirk; "but it wud be no use, an' only losin' of life. The lad be beyont our help or yer gold, either."

"'Tain't de money nor de lands dat'll do, now," moaned Hagar; "it's only de Lord!"

"But think of it, you ungrateful wretches!" cried Trafford, frantically, — "the lad has done more for you and yours than you can ever repay! He went across the sea this time to do you good, and it's for your sakes that he's out in the peril yonder! Will you let him drown without even an attempt to save him? Will you?"

Dirk shook his head. "It be no use," he said, "but we ken try. I be not one to hev it said that I be unthankful. Here, lads, give us a hand! Ef I'll be riskin' my life fur any one, 'tis fur the lad yender."

They dragged a boat down to the curling line of foam, and watching for a favorable opportunity, launched it. Trafford sprang in with them, and they pushed into the darkness. It seemed hardly three minutes to those who stood around the fire, before a great wave came riding in and threw the boat and its load upon the sand. Dirk sprang up and seized Trafford before the returning flood had engulfed him. He pointed to the rent ribs of the boat, saying, as he shook himself,—

"It be as I told ye. Yer lad be beyont yer gold or yer help."

They made no more attempts. Trafford gave up the idea of a rescue, and paced up and down the sand in the very face of the surf that drenched him at every tumble. Utterly helpless! The cold, cruel sea mocked his despair and frenzy. It was great and mighty, and even now was swallowing his treasure, he thought, which lay almost within his power to save. So near!—and yet death between! The thought made him half wild with despair and horror. Yet there was no help,—

nowhere to turn for aid or succor,—not the faintest hope of saving the boy's life. The sea must swallow him.

The fishermen looked askance at the wild, desperate figure that rushed up and down the sand as if it sought to burst through the sea and save its treasure, and whispered gloomily among themselves. Suddenly the man wheeled about and came up to the fire, crying, fiercely,—

"Hagar, you have a God! I cannot find him. Pray to him,—pray to him! Quick, woman!—pray to him before it's too late!"

"Lord help ye, Mas'r Dick!" said Hagar, "I's jes' prayin' fur de dear chile ebery minnit! Don't ye know it? But de Lord's out thar!"—pointing with her skinny finger to the depths of darkness which shrouded the sea, with such vehemence as to startle the fishermen; "he's wid dat boy, and thar can't nuffin kill his soul. It's only goin' to glory quicker'n de rest ob us. Don't ye know it, Mas'r Dick?—can't ye feel it? What's de winds or de waves, so long as de Lord's got ye in his arms, holdin' ye up?—as he's got dat boy ob your'n. Oh, Mas'r Dick! jes' humble yerself 'fore de Lord, right off. What's de use ob stribin' to fight him?—what's de use? 'Tain't no use! —ye knows it dis minnit!—ye knows it all ober! Call on de Lord yerself, Mas'r Dick!—call on de Lord 'fore it's too late!"

"I cannot, I cannot!" groaned Trafford, dropping down on the sand by his old nurse; "I don't know him, and he will not hear me. Oh, my boy, my boy!"

He gave up then. Hagar knew by the way he sank back upon the sand, all the wildness and fierceness gone out of his face, and the crushed, broken-hearted manner in which his head drooped, that he had given up the boy. She gathered his head on her knee, as she had often done when he was a youth, and stroked it tenderly, saying, as her tears dropped,—

"Poor chile, poor honey! Hagar's sorry fur ye. It's a dreadful t'ing not ter know de Lord; ain't it, chile? Can't do nuffin widout him, somehow. But Hagar hopes ye'll find him; she hopes ye'll find him dis berry night. 'Pears like he ain't fur off dis awful night; an', O Lord Jesus!" —folding her hands reverently, and looking toward the sea as if she saw her Redeemer walking there,—"come an' bress dis poor broken heart dat can't find ye.

It's jes' waitin' fur de bressin', an' 'pears like 'twould faint ter def ef ye didn't come. Come, Lord, come."

The night wore slowly on. The "Gull" began to break in pieces and float ashore. The fishermen had enough to do to snatch the boxes and bales which the sea hurled up. As yet, none of the "Gull's" more precious freight of life had made its way through the sea to the shore. Dirk was watching keenly for it. A half-dozen draggled, fearful women had stolen down from their houses, and were standing by the fire, whispering and talking in undertones, with many glances of pity at the figure lying prone on the sand with its head in the old black woman's lap.

"Alack!" said Dirk, with a great sigh, "it wur a fine lad. I never knowed kinder nor better. Ye ken all say that, women, an' this be the sorriest night I ever knowed, 'cept when my little gal died. He wur good to my little gal, the lad wur, an' he giv' me a bit o' flower to put on the sand where she be sleepin', an' it growed an' growed an' blossomed, an' the blossom wur like a great blue eye, —like my little gal's eye,—an' many's the night after fishin' I've gone up ter the buryin'-place ter look at it. An' now the lad himself be gone," said Dirk, wiping his eyes and snuffling.

"Ay, it be a heavy night!" moaned the women, wiping their eyes with the corners of their aprons.

A great heap of bales and boxes and bits of the "Gull's" timbers was accumulating on the sand by the fire. The women sat down on them, keeping up their low talk and whispers, and watching the two silent figures the other side of the fire. The man moved not a muscle. The old negress bent over him, stroking his forehead and whispering and crooning. Only once he had said, chokingly, "My Noll!—all that was left to me," and now lay passive and unheeding, overwhelmed and crushed by the sense of his loss and the consciousness that the sea had quenched the brave, bright life forever.

CHAPTER XXIII.

WAITING.

THE long, long, weary night gave way to a gray and gloomy dawn. The tempest had not abated, and the sea thundered as furiously as ever. The wet and shivering women had gone back to their houses and their little ones; and as the cold, steely light of the coming day began to whiten in the east, Hagar made her way back to her kitchen, where she kindled a fire to warm her numb limbs. Never more, she thought,—rocking to and fro before the pleasant blaze,—could the old house be bright or cheerful. The sea had quenched its life and its joy, and never again would the merry voice echo in the great rooms, or the quick, eager steps sound along the hall and in at her kitchen-door.

"O good, bressed Lord!" moaned she, "bress yer poor chil'en dat's lef' behind! 'Pears like dey was jes' ready ter fall down an' faint ter def ef ye didn't hold 'em up. O Lord, keep Hagar up, an' 'vent her from 'strustin' ye! Bress us, Lord, fur we ain't nuffin dis-yer time. Ye's all we hab ter hold on ter."

Meanwhile, Trafford and the fishermen lingered on the shore, waiting for the sea to give up its dead. The east grew whiter, and light broke dimly over the waste of waves, and faintly showed them where the "Gull" had struck. There was not much left of the little craft, — only a few timbers and the taper point of a mast, wedged in between some outlying rocks, which the sea thundered over. It was a dreary sight, — the vast, immeasurable waste lashed into foam, and dimly discerned through the gray gleaming of the dawn, with the bit of wreck swaying in the waves, where those lives had gone out in the awful thunder and darkness; but Trafford gazed upon it with a calm face. Groans and lamentation could not express the agony which rent his heart, and he walked up and down the drenched sand with a calm, white face that awed Dirk whenever he looked upon it.

"It be a heavier stroke for the master

an' we ken tell, lads," he said to his comrades, as they kept keen lookout for the poor bodies which the sea still kept.

"Ay, there be a heart within him like the rest of us," said one of the fishermen, looking at Trafford as he kept his watchful vigil; "an' he be only losin' what we hev lost afore."

"But the lad wur not like ours," said Dirk, pityingly, "an' it wur a finer lad an' ever I see afore."

So they talked as they watched and waited, and the light grew, and somewhere behind the lowering banks of clouds in the east the sun had risen, and all the land and sea lay cold and warmthless and forlorn. Trafford relinquished not his keen search for a moment, fearful lest the waves should cast his lost treasure at his feet and snatch it back before he could grasp it. The dear face might be bruised and battered by the cruel, remorseless sea, and the eyes could never beam upon him with any light of love or recognition, he thought; yet find it and look upon it he must, even though the sight agonized him. So he watched and waited, with his tearless eyes roaming along the line of foam.

An hour fled. The sea relented, and gave up one poor form into the fishermen's hands. Trafford walked calmly out to where the men were bending over it with pale, awed faces, and saw that it was not Noll. He shivered, looking at the skipper's stalwart figure, and wondered whether, if the sailor but had the power of speech, he might not tell him something of his boy,—whether he met death's dark face calmly and fearlessly, and whether he sent a message to those whom he saw on the shore and could not call to. This thought gave him fresh anguish. If Noll had sent him a farewell, — a last message, — oh, what would he not give to hear it? But, if that were really the case, it had died with those to whom it was intrusted. The sea would never whisper it, — the dead could not. He went back to his lonely pacing.

Another long, long hour passed. The bit of wreck that was jammed between the rocks went to pieces and came ashore. Ben's mate came with it, but no Noll. The men began to straggle homeward, weary and worn with the night's vigil, till only Dirk and Hark Darby were left to keep the stricken master of the stone house company. Oh, such a weary waiting it was! — the ceaseless pouring of the waves upon the sand filling their ears with clamor, and the fearful tide bringing them not the treasure which they sought. Would the sea never give it up? Was the dear form caught and held by the entangling arms of some purple weed in the sea depths? or was it cradled in the calm, unruffled quiet of some crevice of the rocks?

"Oh, cruel, cruel sea!" he cried to himself, "to rob me of my boy, and refuse to give back the poor boon of his body."

It never came. The morning wore on to noon, the noon to night, and still the lonely watcher paced up and down. Toward night the tempest abated, and the turmoil of the sea subsided somewhat. The gray clouds broke and let through a slant mist of yellow sunshine as the sun departed, and the storm was over. Its work was done; and as the clouds fled in ragged squadrons, the calm, untroubled stars shone out over the sea, and mocked, with their deep, unutterable peace, the aching, wretched heart of him who still kept up his lonely pacing. Trafford's eyes suddenly caught sight of their silvery glitter, and he stopped, looking up at them, while the sudden thought flashed through his mind, "Is my boy up there? beyond those shining worlds, in that happy heaven which he trusted in?"

The thought held him silent and motionless. It had not entered his heart before. He had been searching for the lad upon this dreary, sea-beaten shore, without a thought of anything beyond. Was he really standing upon a heavenly shore, where no waves beat nor tempest raved, and, perhaps, looking down upon his own lonely vigil?

There was something in this thought which brought a great calm upon his heart. True, the boy was no less dead nor separated from him; the merry voice was no less hushed to him for all his life and journeying, and the echo of his footsteps might never float down from heavenly paths to gladden his ears; yet, though he realized this, there was a wonderful peace and joy in thinking of the lad as happy and joyous in a sphere where nothing would ever blight his happiness; where he had found those who bore him a great love and had been long waiting for his coming. Trafford sat down on the great pile of broken timbers, and once more looked upward at the stars. Pure and unwavering their gentle eyes looked down at him. And then peaceful as an angel's whisper, came the remembered words of one who was an angel too: "Oh, Richard! don't fail—don't fail to find Him and cling to Him, and come up,—come up too."

Why, oh, why, of all times, did this gentle breathing come to him here? It seemed to Trafford as if his wife's lips had whispered it close to his ear, and he bowed his head upon his breast, while his breath came quick and fast, and bitter tears of grief stood in his eyes. Had God taken his treasures, one after another, and placed them in that heaven which they all looked forward to, that his own wayward, straying heart might be drawn thither? Was this last loss meant to be the great affliction which, through love, should turn his heart toward God and his kingdom? He could not tell; his heart was strangely stirred and melted within him. It seemed to him as if that angel whisper had driven the great burden of despair and agony out of his heart by its gentle breathing, and left it broken and sorrowful, yet not without peace and hope. He looked up at the stars and thought of Noll, and wept. They were not tears of agony, and he did not rave and groan. A slow step came along the sand, turning hither and thither, as if in quest of some one. It drew near Trafford, at last, and a tremulous old voice said,—

"Is dis ye, Mas'r Dick? Hagar's glad 'nough ter find ye, anyhow. 'Pears like she couldn't stay up ter de house, nohow, —'twas so lonesome."

"Yes, I know, Hagar," said the man, without raising his head.

The twilight was so thick that the old negress could not see the speaker's face, but a certain tremble and softness of his voice did not escape her notice.

"Have ye foun' de Lord, Mas'r Dick?" she asked, quickly.

"I know not what I have found," Trafford answered, while his tears fell; "but if I might find his face, and know that it smiled upon me, I should care for little else."

"Now praise de Lord!" said Hagar, fervently; "dat's more'n ye ever felt afore. Thar's help fur ye, Mas'r Dick, an' 'tain't fur off!"

"Too far for me to find it!" said Trafford; "he does not smile upon those who have rejected him."

"Oh, chile!" said Hagar, in a shocked tone; "don't ye know de Lord's all mercy an' lubbin' kin'ness? Don't ye know he won't 'spise an' hate ye jes' as ef he was like a man? Oh, honey! Hagar's feared ter hear ye talk like dat. 'Pears as ef ye made de Lord jes' like poor, eble, good-fur-nuffin man."

Trafford made no reply. A sudden darkness seemed shutting down upon him. It was as if a great golden gleam had fallen out of heaven upon him, warming and softening his heart, and when he turned with tears and joy to look along its pathway heavenward, it vanished and left him groping in confusion and dismay. He got up from off his seat, saying, mournfully,—

"The brightness is all gone from me! I'm in doubt and fear. Oh, how can I ever find his face?—and how can he ever smile upon me who have rejected him?"

Hagar sighed heavily as she said, "Ye don't 'preciate de Lord, chile. Ye talks jes' as ef he was a man, an' could feel 'vengeful towards ye! Don't s'pose any *man* could forgive ye, honey, but de bressed Lord is all lub,—Hagar knows *dat*,—an' Jesus died jes' as much fur ye as he did fur anybody. Ye's got to look to dat bressed Lord Jesus, an' ef ye looks hard 'nough, ye'll find him. Oh, Hagar t'anks de Lord frum de bottom ob her heart fur yer feelin' so to-night."

"But I have not found him! He is hidden from me!" said Trafford.

"But ye will ef ye looks long enough!" said Hagar, cheerfully; "he'll come out ob de darkness to ye, bimeby. Bress ye, chile, dis ole woman was lookin' an' seekin' an' stribin' in mis'ry till she was 'bout ready to give up in 'spair; but I foun' him at las', an' he nebber 'sook Hagar,—nebber!"

The sea was growing calmer with every hour that passed. But it was rough and thunderous still, and its wave-crests gleamed whitely under the starlight. Trafford at last remembered the lateness of the hour, and said, "Come, Hagar, this is no place for us. We will go in."

The two slowly made their way along the shore up to the dark and deserted stone house. Hagar smothered the sigh that rose up from her heart as the silence and loneliness smote upon it, and led the way around to her kitchen-door.

"Poor chile! ye habn't had nuffin to eat dis day," said she, after they were once within her little dominion and she had kindled the fire; "go into de libr'y, honey, an' I'll hab ye sumfin' purty quick."

But Trafford shook his head, saying, "Not there!—not there, yet!" and sat down on the bench by the fire.

Hagar moved wearily about from the cupboard to the table, saying to herself,—

"What ye t'inkin' ob, Hagar, to tell him dat? Dar's all poor Mas'r Noll's books an' t'ings lyin' 'bout eberywhar, an' how ken de poor chile stan' it? De Lord's han' is heaby upon him, an', O good Lord Jesus, jes' come an' bress de poor chile an' sabe him!"

CHAPTER XXIV.

DAYS OF CALM.

HE found it at last, — the peace which comes after a long, weary, despairing struggle. But it was not easily won. It seemed to Trafford as if God had hidden himself in a thick, awful darkness, through which not the faintest ray of light or hope could glimmer upon his heavy, despairing heart. He sought for him as one who, feeling himself in the grasp of Death, would seek for Life. He had long rejected him and put him away; now, in his hour of anguish and extremity, his face and his peace were hard to find. Never had such utter silence reigned in the stone house since its occupancy as reigned there now. Hagar kept mostly within her own province, and Trafford sat day after day in the dining-room, hardly stirring from thence. He had not entered the library since the night of the shipwreck, neither had Hagar stepped within the room, where all Noll's books and shells and treasures gathered from the sea lay, and where everything hinted of the sunny, joyous life which once had made the great room cheerful. Neither looked within, as if they dreaded to recall the dear and pleasant vision of the curly-haired boy who had lived and studied there. These were the days in which Trafford groped in darkness and despondency. Hagar set the table by his side, and brought him his meals, and carried away the untasted viands, with much sighing and regret, but, nevertheless, with joy in her heart.

"'Pears as ef 'twas a drefful t'ing fur de poor chile ter be suff'rin' so," she would sigh to herself as she watched his worn and heavy face on her passages through the room; "but Hagar's t'ankful 'nough to see it, 'cause de poor chile'll find de Lord bimeby. Bress de Lord! Mas'r Dick'll find him some time!"

A long and weary week passed away. Without, the world had never been fairer, nor the sea lovelier. No storms lashed it, and the great world of waves glittered calm and untroubled under the sun, with no hint of death or woe in its purple evening lights or its bright morning gleams.

Then, after this long seeking, a faint hope began to dawn in Trafford's heart. He did not dare to give it heed or trust at first, — he who had been in despair so long, — and when, at last, he began to put forth feeble, trembling anticipations of the peace and joy which might come when God's smile and forgiveness shone upon him, this little ray of hope broadened and grew warmer and brighter, and he began to look up out of his depths of anguish. It was long coming, — it seemed at times to be utterly unattainable, — it was sometimes almost within his heart, and then it fled from him; but at last it came, and abode with him, — this peace which a poor, wandering soul feels after it has found its Lord. Then he was at rest. He came out into Hagar's kitchen one sunshiny afternoon, and, in answer to the old negress' look of wonder and surprise at seeing him there, said, with a grave joy thrilling his words, —

"Hagar, I have found him; and I do not think that his peace will ever leave me, or that my heart will ever forget him."

Hagar got up off the bench where she was sitting, and came slowly forward, saying, brokenly, "Bress de Lord, bress de Lord! dat's all Hagar ken say. Oh, chile, ef ye knew how dis ole heart felt ter hear ye say dem words! ef ye only c'u'd know! But ye nebber will till dis ole woman gits such a tongue as de Lord'll gib her when she gets ter heaben. Den Hagar ken tell ye!"

She followed him to the door, and sat down there in the sunshine, softly blessing him again and again as she watched him follow the thread of a path which led around to the piazza. Trafford paused here, on the smooth sand by the piazza-steps, and looked out upon the sea. It was like a new sea, and the very earth seemed not as of old, for now God reigned over them, and it was his sunshine which fell so brightly and broadly everywhere, and his smile and the knowledge of his forgiveness which filled his heart with such utter peace and tranquillity. This great joy and calm held him quiet for a little space, and, when he turned about, his eyes fell upon the little breadth of grass waving there by the step. One or two gay, crimson asters nodded in the warm wind, planted there by the same hand that watered and cared for the bit of turf. Trafford sat down by them, stroking the turf's green blades, and gazing at the warm-hued flowers through tears.

"Gone — gone," they seemed to whisper as they softly rustled. Somehow these tender, soulless things brought up the boy's memory most vividly. He remembered how Noll sat on the same bit of turf only those two short weeks ago with the warm wind blowing his curly locks about his eyes while he looked off upon the sea. Who thought of danger or death then? Who thought of death lying in wait in that calm, shadowy sea? Trafford's tears fell thick and fast upon the green blades, thinking of the lad. Did ever the sea quench a fairer, brighter life? he wondered, — a life fuller of rich and generous promise? Yet, only two short weeks ago, — short, in reality, but slow and long in passing, — the boy had sat upon this little breadth of verdure full of life and spirits and happiness.

"Ah!" sighed he, "I knew not a treasure I possessed till it passed from me. Now that I have lost it, I see what a blissful life I might have made for myself and it. God forgive me! but I was harsh and cruel to the boy. I made his life darker and less joyous than it ought to have been."

He sat here for a long time, till once more his face was calm and undisturbed. Sometime, he thought, he might meet the boy face to face, and tell him all that his heart longed to unburden itself of. He rose up, at last, and went slowly in, pausing at the library-door. After a few seconds of indecision, he opened it, and went softly in. The room was cold and chilly from its long unoccupancy; but through one of the high windows, and along the floor, streamed a broad bar of cheerful sunlight. It fell right across Noll's study-table and the chair which he was wont to occupy. Trafford moved forward, sat down in the chair, and looked about him with misty eyes. Traces of the boy's presence everywhere! The familiar school-books, open to the last lessons which Trafford had heard him recite; bits of paper, with sums and solutions traced thereon; copies of the fine and feathery sea-moss, which it was the boy's delight to gather, with odd pebbles and shells, met his gaze on either hand. He took up a scrap of paper from among the rest, and found something thereon which the boy had written, evidently in an idle moment. Trafford, however, read it not without emotion. It merely said:—

"*Wednes., Aug. 24.*—This is a long, gray, rainy day, and I have not stirred out of the house. I am at this moment (or ought to be) studying my Latin lesson. Uncle Richard has not spoken a word to me since breakfast. I wish I knew what made him look so grim and sober to-day, and I *do* wish he would speak to me. When the fog lifted just now, I fancied I saw a ship on the horizon, bound for Hastings, I suppose. Oh, but I —"

Here the slight record was broken off. Perhaps the boy had gone back to his Latin, or perhaps the passing ship had taken his thoughts along with it to Hastings, and thus left the half-commenced exclamation unfinished. Trafford read and reread the little bit of paper, and folded it carefully, and put it away with the precious letter which the boy's father had written on his dying-bed. Then he began to gather up Noll's books, thinking to put them out of his sight, but stopped before he had taken the third in his hand. Why hide them? Why shut them up in darkness, as if some evil, dreaded memory were connected with the sight of them? Had not everything about the boy and his life been bright and pleasant to think of? He put the books back in their places, saying to himself, "They shall stay where they are. Hagar shall not move them, and I will have them before my eyes alway, just as his dear hands left them? Why should I try to hide aught that his blessed memory lingers around?"

So he left everything just as Noll's hands had placed them last, and rose up from his chair, and went to his old familiar seat by the great bookcase, where he had sat and pored over great volumes day after day, and watched the boy at his studies. The portrait on the wall looked down at him with its soft and tender eyes, and he thought, "Now I may look at it without its reproaching me; for, dear heart, I have begun to 'come up.' I have turned my eyes toward thy abode, and, God helping me, I may some day hear thy own sweet voice. And though I may never see the boy's face, and rejoice to look upon it as I do upon thine, yet his pure memory lingers about everything that he loved and touched, and his face can never be removed from my heart."

Calm and peaceful days passed, and the third week after the shipwreck went by, and life in the stone house began to move on as it was wont to do. Once more the red light from the library-window streamed out into the night, but there was no Skipper Ben and his "Gull" for it to guide. Not a sail had been seen near the Rock, and its inhabitants had been shut out from the rest of mankind for three long weeks. That which at first was only an inconvenience grew to be a serious matter at last. The Culm folk, never very provident, exhausted their supply of flour and meal, and had only fish to eat; and fish, with a little salt, was not an extensive nor varied bill of fare.

In some way or another, Hagar discovered that the people had exhausted all their stores, and through her it came to Trafford's ears.

"Nuffin but fish ter live on, an' not de greatest plenty o' dat," Hagar had said, standing beside Trafford's chair in the library.

The man started, as a sudden remembrance of forgotten duties came into his mind. He had neglected to look after those Culm people, — he had forgotten about Noll's school and its pupils. But it should be so no longer, he resolved at once. That work which the boy loved and desired to complete, he would take up and carry out. It should be a pleasure and delight. He would gather up the broken, half-completed plans, and make it the work of his life to perfect them as Noll would have done. Now the inmates of the stone house were not well supplied with provisions, as the winter stores had not been laid in. There was no telling when another ship would touch at Culm, but, in all probability, it would be soon. The skipper must have friends somewhere, who would be searching for his whereabouts. Trafford divided his supplies with the fishermen, trusting that ere long some sail would appear, bound for the Rock, or within signalling distance of it. He walked often by the sea, looking toward Hastings, and trying in vain to discern some sail bound hitherward. He walked over to Culm village, and lingered about the little room where Noll's school had been, and resolved that the plan of a new schoolroom, with good seats, benches, and a faithful teacher, should be carried out if ever communication was opened between the Rock and Hastings. And if no teacher could be got for the winter, he would teach the children himself. He wondered whether there were any chairs or benches left from the cargo of the "Gull," remembering that Noll was to bring school-furniture from Hastings with him; but, though he searched long and keenly among the timbers and refuse which the sea had thrown up, he could not find so much as a bit of varnished wood that looked as if it might have belonged to a desk or chair. At this he wondered, but thought, "The poor boy was unsuccessful, or else the sea refuses to give up aught that was his, as well as himself."

And still he watched and waited for a sail, thinking that if none came soon, a way must be devised for getting to Hastings.

CHAPTER XXV.

OUT OF THE SEA.

THE fourth week after the shipwreck dragged slowly away, — spent in watching and waiting for a sail. None came. The lack of good food was getting to be a serious matter for both Culm folk and the inmates of the stone house. Trafford's stores were well-nigh exhausted, and the last day of that long fourth week was spent in company with Dirk Sharp and some of his comrades, devising plans by which they might communicate with Hastings. The master of the stone house walked homeward after his conference with the fishermen, and paused in the gathering dusk on the spot where he had stood that fearful night when the "Gull" and her crew were on the rocks in the awful roar and thunder of the tempest. How silent and peaceful it all lay now, — the sea purpling in its calm and shadowy depths, its waves faintly murmuring on the pebbles, and, overhead, the arch of silvery sky bending down to the far horizon, full of the tender lights of the after-glow! Only one month since that fearful night, yet how far in the dim past the event seemed! What a great darkness and despair he had struggled through! How full and real every minute of those four weeks had been! And, as he stood there, such strong and tender memories of the lad he had lost came back to him that he turned away with a throbbing heart, and walked homeward along the sand with a bowed head, and so failed to see the white gleaming of a sail which rose out of the sea and stood toward the Rock. The lingering daylight touched it with a rosy flush as the rising night-breeze bore it steadily onward; but Trafford saw it not, and went up the piazza-steps, and into the stone house, without turning his eyes seaward.

He ate his scanty supper, which Hagar — poor heart! — had placed upon the table with a wonderful display of dishes, as if to make up for the lack of food by a board spread with cups and plates enough for a feast, and then took his way to the silent library. He sat down at his organ, and from its long-silent pipes drew soft and tender music that filled the room and stole gently through the house. The tears came into Hagar's eyes as she listened to it.

"'Pears as ef de angels was singin'," she said, wiping her cheeks. "Hagar wonders ef de Lord'll gib her a voice like dat when she gets ter glory."

It died away at last in gentle, tremulous whispers, and Trafford walked to the window and looked out. Twilight had settled so thickly that the sea was quite hidden, save a faint glimmer of ripples along the sand. Deep quiet reigned over land and sea, and nowhere with such undisputed sway as in the stone house. Trafford lit his study-lamp and sat down, with no desire, however, to read or study.

Hardly had he seated himself, when, with startling suddenness, a shrill scream broke upon the deep quiet. It was Hagar's voice, and the cry came from her kitchen; and before Trafford had recovered from his surprise, there was a little sound of commotion in her distant province,—doors were thrown open, voices echoed, and then along the silent hall came a sound — the rush of eager feet — that drove every trace of color from Trafford's face, as well it might, and made his heart beat so loud and wildly that he pressed his hands over it to stay its tumultuous beating. He started up, gazing with wide-open eyes at the library-door, while at every echo of those coming footsteps, he started and trembled, and grew faint with anticipation. The door burst open, and there stood—Noll Trafford!

"It's I, Uncle Richard" Page 421.

One moment the boy paused, perhaps frightened by the white face of the man who sat gazing motionlessly at him, then he bounded forward, crying, "It's I, Uncle Richard! — your own Noll!"

Trafford's arms did not clasp the boy about; his tongue refused to articulate; his heart could not take in this great, overwhelming joy. But Noll's arms were about his neck, the boy's warm breath was upon his cheek, and in his ears was the lad's whisper, "It's I, — I, Uncle Richard! no one else!"

Then the man began to sigh, just as if he were awakening from a long and troubled dream, and presently he put out his hand and touched the boy's cheeks, as if to assure himself that it was not all a vision, and then he said, chokingly, "My boy, — *mine!* O God! I don't deserve this."

His arms clasped the lad in one long, fervent embrace. He bent his head over the curly locks, and wept for joy, stroking the lad's shoulders and pressing his hands the while, as if he were not yet sure that the boy was a reality. He looked upon him as one from the dead. Had the sea given him up?—had that terrible tempest spared him in its wild fury? Why had the boy lingered so long? Where had he been sojourning all these long weeks? But too happy in the consciousness that it was really Noll, safe and unharmed, who was before him, to care for aught further at present, he sat silently holding the boy's hands, while his heart gave grateful thanks to God.

"Poor Uncle Richard!" said the boy, at last.

Trafford's lips moved, and with an effort

he said, "No, no,—not *poor!* I'm rich, rich!—*so* rich! O God, help me! I can't believe my own happiness."

"But it's really I, Uncle Richard!" said Noll, assuringly; "you've felt my hands, my face, my shoulders, and aren't they alive and warm?"

"Yes, it is really you, thank God!" said Trafford, drawing a long breath, while he gazed upon the merry face that he never more expected to see on earth.

"Yes, and oh, Uncle Richard, you can't know how I longed to see you, to tell you that I was alive and safe! I knew you would worry, but I didn't think you'd think me dead. I didn't think *that* till we got to Culm, and Dirk and all the rest trembled, and were actually going to run away from me!"

"Then you have not been harmed?"

said Trafford; "but oh, my boy, where were you on that awful night?"

"Safe and sound, with Ned Thorn, at Hastings, Uncle Richard, and not even dreaming of danger or shipwreck. You see, the furniture was not ready, and I hadn't found a teacher, and so I stayed. Ned and I went down to the wharf the night before the 'Gull' was to sail, and carried a letter to the skipper to give to you, telling you why I couldn't come; but poor Ben never got here alive, and the letter was lost with him, I suppose. Oh, Uncle Richard, if I *had* started,—if the furniture had been ready—"

"Thank God it was not!" interrupted Trafford, presently; "he watched over you, he stayed your coming, and now he has brought you out of the sea, as it were, to me. Oh, Noll!"

The boy looked up eagerly. "Have—have you found the Lord Jesus, Uncle Richard?" he asked.

Trafford's hands rested tenderly on the boy's head. "Yes," he said, with a great calm and peace in his voice, "I found him through great sorrow and grief. I think God led me through all this suffering that my heart might be softened and turned toward him. And now this Saviour has brought you back to me!"

A deep silence followed, full of unutterable joy. Trafford reverently bent his head, his lips quivering with emotion, and with his nephew's hands clasped in his, silently thanked God for his goodness, for this great joy which was come into his life, for this precious lad that was dead and now was alive again. It seemed as if God had brought him out of the sea to him. At last Noll said, taking up his explanation where he had left it off,—

"After we had given the letter to the skipper, I thought no more about it, and Ned and I were busy enough with seeing about the furniture for a day or two, and we didn't notice the storm, or even think of the 'Gull' being in danger. And Mr. Gray helped me to find a teacher, and we were so busy with plans that the time passed away before I knew it, and when I came to go down on the wharf to engage a passage with Ben, the men said the 'Gull' had never got back from her last trip, and they were afraid it was lost. Ned didn't believe there had been a shipwreck, neither did Mr. Gray. He said that most likely the skipper had been kept by some business, or perhaps the 'Gull' had gone further down the coast than usual. Oh, Uncle Richard! we didn't think that poor Ben was drowned, nor that you thought me wrecked with him."

Trafford said, "Those were fearful days for me. Go on, go on, Noll."

"We went down to the wharf every night till another week was gone, and then we began to be certain that Ben was either wrecked or sick, and I began to be anxious to get some word to you. I thought that perhaps you might be worried about me, though Mr. Gray said that if the 'Gull' was wrecked anywhere near Culm, you could not help but know I was not on board. We waited and waited till the three weeks were gone, and then some of Ben's friends began to talk of going in search of him. But it was only till last night that they were ready to go, and we came off before daylight this morning. Oh, the time has seemed so long, Uncle Richard! but here I am, safe and sound, once more."

Trafford looked at his nephew as if he could yet hardly believe his eyes.

"And you should have seen Dirk and the rest!" continued Noll; "why, he wouldn't speak to me at first, but was going to run away; but when he did find that it was really I, he cried like a great child. He said that you thought me dead, —you can't know how I felt when he said that, Uncle Richard,—and so Ned and I didn't wait any longer, but ran all the way here. I can think, now, why you looked so white when I came in at the door!"

Trafford stroked the boy's hair, saying, "I never thought to hear the echoes of your feet again, God knows. Oh, my boy, *you* can never know what this night has brought to me. He who led you thither only can. But whose name did you mention?"

"Ned's; he came down with me, Uncle Richard, for it's vacation at Hastings. We came up to the kitchen-door, because Hagar's light shone so brightly, and what do you think? she threw up her hands and screamed at the sight of me. But it didn't take long to make her certain that I was real, and not a vision. And, oh, there's one thing I'd forgotten! The new teacher is at Culm, waiting for Dirk to come over with his trunks. It's one of papa's old scholars, Uncle Richard, and his name is Henry Fields. He worked with papa in the old sea-town where we lived, and he's come down to work here at Culm among our fish-folk. I like him very much, and you can't help but like him, too; and we've brought a cargo of benches and desks all ready to —"

The library-door began to swing softly open, — not so softly, however, but that Noll heard and stopped.

"It's Ned," he said, looking over his shoulder. "Come in!"

Ned came shyly around to where they were sitting, his usually merry face sobered by something which he perceived in the faces of his friends before him. A silence fell upon them here. Ned leaned against his friend, looking soberly at Trafford's rapt face, and wondering where all the man's grimness and gloominess had gone. And just then a sudden thought came into Noll's heart, and he said, looking up brightly, —

"It's a year this very night since I

came to you, Uncle Richard! Don't you remember? What a long, long time!"

Trafford said, "Yes, I remember. Through all the days since then God has been teaching me, and he has led me on to this; and, oh! my boy, the sea may never divide us again, for, though through its dark floods we go down to death, beyond there is light and God and heaven!" And in his voice there was peace unutterable.

If this Story of a Year, and what it taught, is not already too long, you may know that a schoolhouse was built at Culm, and that Henry Fields proved a good and faithful teacher; that a stanch, new "White Gull" was built, and one of Skipper Ben's sea-loving sons was its captain; that the Culm children and their parents slowly improved in more ways than one under the constant, unfailing care and effort of Trafford and his nephew; that the Rock was not always Noll Trafford's home, but exchanged for a pleasanter one in Hastings, though the old stone house was often brightened by his presence, and never got to be entirely gloomy and deserted again.

www.ingramcontent.com/pod-product-compliance
Lightning Source LLC
LaVergne TN
LVHW021137110826
845150LV00005B/1050